FORDING THE CHAMELICON RIVER

THREE GRINGOS
IN VENEZUELA AND
CENTRAL AMERICA

BY

RICHARD HARDING DAVIS

ILLUSTRATED

Fredonia Books
Amsterdam, The Netherlands

Three Gringos in Venezuela and Central America

by
Richard Harding Davis

ISBN: 1-58963-902-2

Copyright © 2002 by Fredonia Books

Reprinted from the 1904 edition

Fredonia Books
Amsterdam, The Netherlands
http://www.fredoniabooks.com

TO

MY FRIENDS

H. SOMERS SOMERSET

AND

LLOYD GRISCOM

CONTENTS

ILLUSTRATIONS

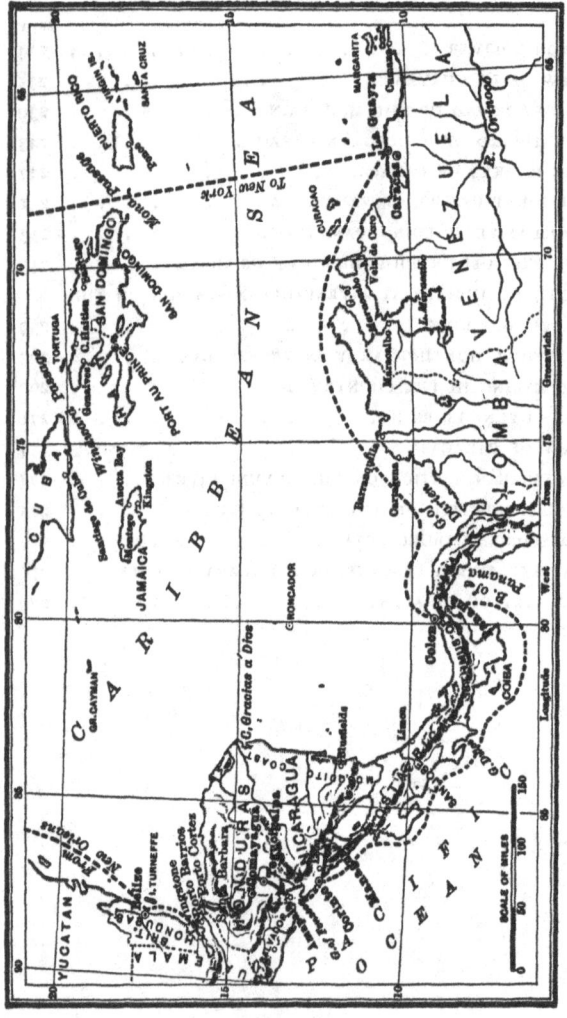

MAP OF VENEZUELA AND CENTRAL AMERICA, SHOWING THE ROUTE OF THE "THREE GRINGOS"

ON THE CARIBBEAN SEA

THE steamer *Breakwater* lay at the end of a muddy fruit-wharf a mile down the levee.

She was listed to sail that morning for Central American ports, and we were going with her in search of warm weather and other unusual things. When we left New York the streets were lined with frozen barricades of snow, upon which the new brooms of a still newer administration had made so little impression that people were using them as an excuse for being late for dinners; and at Washington, while the snow had disappeared, it was still bitterly cold. And now even as far south as New Orleans we were shivering in our great-coats, and the newspapers were telling of a man who, the night before, had been found frozen to death in the streets. It seemed as though we were to keep on going south, forever seeking warmth, only to find that Nature at every point of lower latitude had paid us the compliment of changing her season to spite us.

So the first question we asked when we came over the side of the *Breakwater* was not when we should first see land, but when we should reach warm weather.

There were four of us, counting Charlwood, young Somerset's servant.   There was Henry Somers Somerset, who has travelled greater distances for a boy still under age than any other one of his much-travelled countrymen that I have ever met.   He has covered as many miles in the last four years as would make five trips around the world, and he came with me for the fun of it, and in what proved the vain ·hope of big game.   The third was Lloyd Griscom, of Philadelphia, and later of London, where he has been attaché at our embassy during the present administration.   He had been ordered south by his doctor, and only joined us the day before we sailed.

We sat shivering under the awning on the upper deck, and watched the levees drop away on either side as we pushed down the last ninety miles of the Mississippi River.   Church spires and the roofs of houses showed from the low-lying grounds behind the dikes, and gave us the impression that we were riding on an elevated road.   The great river steamers, with paddle-wheels astern and high double smoke-stacks, that were associated in our minds with pictures of the war and those in our school geographies, passed us, pouring out heavy volumes of black smoke, on their way to St. Louis, and on each bank we recognized, also from pictures, magnolia-trees and the ugly cotton-gins and the rows of negroes' quarters like the men's barracks in a fort.

At six o'clock, when we had reached the Gulf, the sun sank a blood-red disk into great desolate bayous of long grass and dreary stretches of vacant water. Dead trees with hanging gray moss and mistletoe on their bare branches reared themselves out of the swamps like gallows-trees or giant sign-posts pointing the road to nowhere; and the herons, perched by dozens on their limbs or moving heavily across the sky with harsh, melancholy cries, were the only signs of life. On each side of the muddy Mississippi the waste swampland stretched as far as the eye could reach, and every blade of the long grass and of the stunted willows and every post of the dikes stood out black against the red sky as vividly as though it were lit by a great conflagration, and the stagnant pools and stretches of water showed one moment like flashing lakes of fire, and the next, as the light left them, turned into mirrors of ink. It was a scene of the most awful and beautiful desolation, and the silence, save for the steady breathing of the steamer's engine, was the silence of the Nile at night.

For the next three days we dropped due south as the map lies from the delta of the Mississippi through the Gulf of Mexico to the Caribbean Sea. It was moonlight by night, and sun and blue water by day, and the decks kept level, and the vessel was clean.

Our fellow-passengers were banana-planters and engineers going to Panama and Bluefields, and we asked them many questions concerning rates of exchange and the rainy season and distances and means of transportation, to which they gave answers as opposite as can only come from people who have lived together in the same place for the greater part of their lives.

Land, when it came, appeared in the shape of little islands that floated in mid-air above the horizon like the tops of trees, without trunks to support them, or low-lying clouds. They formed the skirmish-line of Yucatan, the northern spur of Central America, and seemed from our decks as innocent as the Jersey sand-hills, but were, the pilot told us, inhabited by wild Indians who massacre people who are so unfortunate as to be shipwrecked there, and who will not pay taxes to Mexico. But the little we saw of their savagery was when we passed within a ship's length of a ruined temple to the Sun, standing conspicuously on a jutting point of land, with pillars as regular and heavily cut as some of those on the Parthenon. It was interesting to find such a monument a few days out from New Orleans.

Islands of palms on one side and blue mountains on the other, and water as green as corroded copper, took the place of the white sandbanks of Yucatan, and on the third day out we had passed the Mexican state and steamed in towards the coast of British Honduras, and its chief seaport and capital, Belize.

British Honduras was formerly owned by Spain, as was all of Central America, and was, on account of its bays and islands, a picturesque refuge for English and other pirates. In the seventeenth century English logwood-cutters visited the place and obtained a footing, which has been extended since by concessions and by conquest, so that the place is now a British dependency. It forms a little slice of land between Yucatan and Guatemala, one hundred and seventy-four miles in its greatest length, and running sixty-eight miles inland.

Belize is a pretty village of six thousand people, living in low, broad-roofed bungalows, lying white and cool-looking in the border of waving cocoanut-trees and tall, graceful palms. It was not necessary to tell us that Belize would be the last civilized city we should see until we reached the capital of Spanish Honduras. A British colony is always civilized; it is always the same, no matter in what latitude it may be, and it is al-

ways distinctly British. Every one knows that
an Englishman takes his atmosphere with him
wherever he goes, but the truth of it never impressed me so much as it did at Belize. There
were not more than two hundred English men
and women in the place, and yet, in the two
halves of two days that I was there I seemed to
see everything characteristic of an Englishman
in his native land. There were a few concessions
made to the country and to the huge native population, who are British subjects themselves; but
the colony, in spite of its surroundings, was just
as individually English as is the shilling that the
ship's steward pulls out of his pocket with a
handful of the queer coin that he has picked up
at the ports of a half-dozen Spanish republics.
They may be of all sizes and designs, and of
varying degrees of a value, or the lack of it,
which changes from day to day, but the English
shilling, with the queen's profile on one side and
its simple " one shilling " on the other, is worth
just as much at that moment and at that distance from home as it would be were you hand-
ing it to a hansom-cab driver in Piccadilly. And
we were not at all surprised to find that the
black native police wore the familiar blue-and-
white-striped cuff of the London bobby, and the
district-attorney a mortar-board cap and gown,
and the colonial bishop gaiters and an apron.
It was quite in keeping, also, that the advertise-

GOVERNMENT HOUSE. BELIZE

ments on the boardings should announce and give equal prominence to a "Sunday-school treat" and a boxing-match between men of H.M.S. *Pelican*, and that the officers of that man-of-war should be playing cricket with a local eleven under the full tropical sun, and that the chairs in the Council-room and Government House should be of heavy leather stamped V.R., with a crown above the initials. An American official in as hot a climate, being more adaptable, would have had bamboo chairs with large, open-work backs, or would have even supplied the council with rocking-chairs.

Lightfoot agreed to take us ashore at a quarter of a dollar apiece. He had a large open sail-boat, and everybody called him Lightfoot and seemed to know him intimately, so we called him Light-foot too. He was very black, and light-hearted at least, and spoke English with the soft, hesitating gentleness that marks the speech of all these natives. It was Sunday on land, and Sunday in an English colony is observed exactly as it should be, and so the natives were in heavily starched white clothes, and were all apparently going somewhere to church in rigid rows of five or six. But there were some black soldiers of the West India Regiment in smart Zouave uniforms and turbans that furnished us with local color, and we pursued one of them for some time admiringly, until he become nervous and beat a retreat to the barracks.

Somerset had a letter from his ambassador in
Washington to Sir Alfred Moloney, K.C.M.G.,
the governor of British Honduras, and as we
hoped it would get us all an invitation to dinner,

SIR ALFRED MOLONEY
(Central Figure)

we urged him to present it at once. Four days
of the ship's steward's bountiful dinners, served
at four o'clock in the afternoon, had made us
anxious for a change both in the hour and the

diet. The governor's house at Belize is a very large building, fronting the bay, with one of the finest views from and most refreshing breezes on its veranda that a man could hope to find on a warm day, and there is a proud and haughty sentry at each corner of the grounds and at the main entrance. A fine view of blue waters beyond a green turf terrace covered with cannon and lawn-tennis courts, and four sentries marching up and down in the hot sun, ought to make any man, so it seems to me, content to sit on his porch in the shade and feel glad that he is a governor.

Somerset passed the first sentry with safety, and we sat down on the grass by the side of the road opposite to await developments, and were distressed to observe him make directly for the kitchen, with the ambassador's letter held firmly in his hand. So we stood up and shouted to him to go the other way, and he became embarrassed, and continued to march up and down the gravel walk with much indecision, and as if he could not make up his mind where he wanted to go, like the grenadiers in front of St. James's Palace. It happened that his excellency was out, so Somerset left our cards and his letter, and we walked off through the green, well-kept streets and wondered at the parrots and the chained monkeys and the Anglicized little negro girls in white cotton stockings and with Sunday-school books under their arms. All the show-places of interest were closed on that day, so, after an ineffectual attempt to force our way into the jail, which we mistook for a monastery, we walked back through an avenue of cocoanut-palms to the International Hotel for dinner.

We had agreed that as it was our first dinner on shore, it should be a long and excellent one, with several kinds of wine. The International Hotel is a large one, with four stories, and a balcony on each floor; and after wandering over the first three of these in the dark we came upon a lonely woman with three crying children, who told us with reproving firmness that in Belize the dinner-hour is at four in the afternoon, and that no one should expect a dinner at seven. We were naturally cast down at this rebuff, and even more so when her husband appeared out of the night and informed us that keeping a hotel did not pay—at least, that it did not pay him—and that he could not give us anything to drink because he had not renewed his license, and even if he had a license he would not sell us anything on Sunday. He had a touch of malaria, he said, and took a gloomy view of life in consequence, and our anxiety to dine well seemed, in contrast, unfeeling and impertinent. But we praised the beauty of the three children, and did not set him right when he mistook us for officers from the English gunboats in the harbor, and for one of

NATIVE CONSTABULARY. BELIZE.

these reasons he finally gave us a cold dinner by the light of a smoking lamp, and made us a present of a bottle of stout, for which he later refused any money. We would have enjoyed our dinner at Belize in spite of our disappointment had not an orderly arrived in hot search after Somerset, and borne him away to dine at Government House, where Griscom and I pictured him, as we continued eating our cold chicken and beans, dining at her majesty's expense, with fine linen and champagne, and probably ice. Lightfoot took us back to the boat in mournful silence, and we spent the rest of the evening on the quarter-deck telling each other of the most important people with whom we had ever dined, and had nearly succeeded in re-establishing our self-esteem, when Somerset dashed up in a man-of-war's launch glittering with brass and union-jacks, and left it with much ringing of electric bells and saluting and genial farewells from admirals and midshipmen in gold-lace, with whom he seemed to be on a most familiar and friendly footing. This was the final straw, and we held him struggling over the ship's side, and threatened to drop him to the sharks unless he promised never to so desert us again. And discipline was only restored when he assured us that he was the bearer of an invitation from the governor to both breakfast and luncheon the following morning. The governor apologized the next day for the in-

formality of the manner in which he had sent us
the invitation, so I thought it best not to tell
him that it had been delivered by a young man
while dangling by his ankles from the side of the
ship, with one hand holding his helmet and the
other clutching at the rail of the gangway.

There is much to be said of Belize, for in its
way it was one of the prettiest ports at which
we touched, and its cleanliness and order, while
they were not picturesque or foreign to us then,
were in so great contrast to the ports we visited
later as to make them most remarkable.   It was
interesting to see the responsibilities and the
labor of government apportioned out so carefully
and discreetly, and to find commissioners of
roads, and then district commissioners, and under
them inspectors, and to hear of boards of education and boards of justice, each doing its ap-
pointed work in this miniature government, and
all responsible to the representative of the big
government across the sea.   And it was reassur-
ing to read in the blue-books of the colony that
the health of the port has improved enormously
during the last three years.

Monday showed an almost entirely different
Belize from the one we had seen on the day
before.   Shops were open and busy, and the
markets were piled high with yellow oranges and
bananas and strange fruits, presided over by
negresses in rich-colored robes and turbans, and

MAIN STREET, BELIZE

smoking fat cigars. There was a show of justice also in a parade of prisoners, who, in spite of their handcuffs, were very anxious to halt long enough to be photographed, and there was a great bustle along the wharves, where huge rafts of logwood and mahogany floated far into the water. The governor showed us through his botanical station, in which he has collected food-giving products from over all the world, and plants that absorb the malaria in the air, and he hinted at the social life of Belize as well, tempting us with a ball and dinners to the officers of the men-of-war; but the *Breakwater* would not wait for such frivolities, so we said farewell to Belize and her kindly governor, and thereafter walked under strange flags, and were met at every step with the despotic little rules and safeguards which mark unstable governments.

Livingston was like a village on the coast of East Africa in comparison with Belize. It is the chief seaport of Guatemala on the Atlantic side, and Guatemala is the furthest advanced of all the Central American republics; but her civilization lies on the Pacific side, and does not extend so far as her eastern boundary.

There are two opposite features of landscape in the tropics which are always found together—the royal palm, which is one of the most beautiful of things, and the corrugated zinc-roof custom-house, which is one of the ugliest. Nature

NATIVE WOMEN AT LIVINGSTON

never appears so extravagant or so luxurious as she does in these hot latitudes; but just as soon as she has fashioned a harbor after her own liking, and set it off at her best so that it is a haven of delight to those who approach it from the sea, civilized man comes along and hammers square walls of zinc together and spoils the beauty of the place forever.   The natives, who do not care for customs dues, help nature out with thatch-roofed huts and walls of adobe or yellow cane, or add curved red tiles to the more pretentious houses, and so fill out the picture. But the "gringo," or the man from the interior, is in a hurry, and wants something that will withstand earthquakes and cyclones, and so wherever you go you can tell that he has been there before you by his architecture of zinc.

When you turn your back on the custom-house at Livingston and the rows of wooden shops with open fronts, you mount the hill upon which the town stands, and there you will find no houses but those which have been created out of the mud and the trees of the place itself. There are no streets to the village nor doors to the houses; they are all exactly alike, and the bare mud floor of one is as unindividual, except for the number of naked children crawling upon it, as is any of the others. The sun and the rain are apparently free to come and go as they like, and every one seems to live in the back of the house, under the thatched roof which shades the clay ovens. Most of the natives were coal-black, and the women, in spite of the earth floors below and the earth walls round about them, were clean, and wore white gowns that trailed from far down their arms, leaving the chest and shoulders bare. They were a very simple, friendly lot of people, and ran from all parts of the settlement to be photographed, and brought us flowers from their gardens, for which they refused money.

We had our first view of the Central American soldier at Livingston, and, in spite of all we had heard, he surprised us very much. The oldest of those whom we saw was eighteen years, and the youngest soldiers were about nine. They wore blue jean uniforms, ornamented with white tape, and the uniforms differed in shade according to the number of times they had been washed. These young men carried their muskets half-way up the barrel, or by the bayonet, dragging the stock on the ground.

General Barrios, the young President of Guatemala, has some very smart soldiers at the capital, and dresses them in German uniforms, which is a compliment he pays to the young German emperor, for whom he has a great admiration; but his discipline does not extend so far as the Caribbean Sea.

The river Dulce goes in from Livingston, and we were told it was one of the things in Central America we ought to see, as its palisades were more beautiful than those of the Rhine. The man who told us this said he spoke from hearsay, and that he had never been on the Rhine, but that he knew a gentleman who had. You can well believe that it is very beautiful from what you can see of its mouth, where it flows into the Caribbean between great dark banks as

THE GUATEMALLECAN ARMY AT LIVINGSTON

high as the palisades opposite Dobbs Ferry, and covered with thick, impenetrable green.

Port Barrios, to which one comes in a few hours, is at one end of a railroad, and surrounded by all the desecration that such an improvement on nature implies, in the form of zinc depots, piles of railroad-ties, and rusty locomotives. The town consists of a single row of native huts along the coast, terminating in a hospital. Every house is papered throughout with copies of the New York *Police Gazette*, which must give the Guatemallecan a lurid light on the habits and virtues of his cousins in North

BARRACKS AT PORT BARRIOS

America. Most of our passengers left the ship here, and we met them, while she was taking on bananas, wandering about the place with blank faces, or smiling grimly at the fate which condemned them and their blue-prints and transits to a place where all nature was beautiful and only civilized man was discontented.

We lay at Barrios until late at night, wandering round the deserted decks, or watching the sharks sliding through the phosphorus and the lights burning in the huts along the shore. At midnight we weighed anchor, and in the morning steamed into Puerto Cortez, the chief port of Spanish Honduras, where the first part of our journey ended, and where we exchanged the ship's deck for the Mexican saddle, and hardtack for tortillas.

THE EXILED LOTTERY

WO years ago, while I was passing through Texas, I asked a young man in the smoking-car if he happened to know where I could find the United States troops, who were at that time riding somewhere along the borders of Texas and Mexico, and engaged in suppressing the so-called Garza revolution.

The young man did not show, that he was either amused or surprised at the abruptness of the question, but answered me promptly, as a matter of course, and with minute detail. "You want to go to San Antonio," he said, "and take the train to Laredo, on the Mexican boundary, and then change to the freight that leaves once a day to Corpus Christi, and get off at Pena station. Pena is only a water-tank, but you can hire a horse there and ride to the San Rosario Ranch. Captain Hardie is at Rosario with Troop G, Third Cavalry. They call him the Riding

Captain, and if any one can show you all there is to see in this Garza outfit, he can."

The locomotive whistle sounded at that moment, the train bumped itself into a full stop at a station, and the young man rose. "Goodday," he said, smiling pleasantly; "I get off here."

He was such an authoritative young man, and he had spoken in so explicit a manner, that I did as he had directed; and if the story that followed was not interesting, the fault was mine, and not that of my chance adviser.

A few months ago I was dining alone in Delmonico's, when the same young man passed out through the room, and stopped on his way beside my table.

"Do you remember me?" he said. "I met you once in a smoking-car in Texas. Well, I've got a story now that's better than any you'll find lying around here in New York. You want to go to a little bay called Puerto Cortez, on the eastern coast of Honduras, in Central America, and look over the exiled Louisiana State Lottery there. It used to be the biggest gambling concern in the world, but now it's been banished to a single house on a mud-bank covered with palm-trees, and from there it reaches out all over the United States, and sucks in thousands and thousands of victims like a great octopus. You want to go there and write a story about it. Good-night," he added; then he nodded again, with a smile, and walked across the room and disappeared into Broadway.

When a man that you have met once in a smoking-car interrupts you between courses to suggest that you are wasting your time in New York, and that you ought to go to a coral reef in Central America and write a story of an outlawed lottery, it naturally interests you, even if it does not spoil your dinner. It interested me, at least, so much that I went back to my rooms at once, and tried to find Puerto Cortez on the map; and later, when the cold weather set in, and the grass-plots in Madison Square turned into piled-up islands of snow, surrounded by seas of slippery asphalt, I remembered the palm-trees, and went South to investigate the exiled lottery. That is how this chapter and this book came to be written.

Every one who goes to any theatre in the United States may have read among the adver-tisements on the programme an oddly worded one which begins, "Conrad! Conrad! Conrad!" and which goes on to say that—

"In accepting the Presidency of the Honduras Na-tional Lottery Company (Louisiana State Lottery Com-pany) I shall not surrender the Presidency of the Gulf Coast Ice and Manufacturing Company, of Bay St. Louis, Miss.

"Therefore address all proposals for supplies, machinery, etc., as well as all business communications, to
"PAUL CONRAD, Puerto Cortez, Honduras,
    "Care Central America Express,
                "FORT TAMPA CITY,
                    "FLORIDA, U. S. A."

You have probably read this advertisement
often, and enjoyed the naïve manner in which Mr.
Conrad asks for correspondence on different subjects, especially on that relating to "all business
communications," and how at the same time he
has so described his whereabouts that no letters
so addressed would ever reach his far-away home
in Puerto Cortez, but would be promptly stopped
at Tampa, as he means that they should.

After my anonymous friend had told me of
Puerto Cortez, I read of it on the programme
with a keener interest, and Puerto Cortez became
to me a harbor of much mysterious moment, of
a certain dark significance, and of possible adventure. I remembered all that the lottery had
been before the days of its banishment, and all
that it had dared to be when, as a corporation
legally chartered by the State of Louisiana, it
had put its chain and collar upon legislatures
and senators, judges and editors, when it had
silenced the voice of the church and the pulpit
by great gifts of money to charities and hospi-
tals, so giving out in a lump sum with one hand
what it had taken from the people in dollars and

half-dollars, five hundred and six hundred fold, with the other. I remembered when its trademark, in open-faced type, " La. S. L.," was as familiar in every newspaper in the United States as were the names of the papers themselves, when it had not been excommunicated by the postmaster-general, and it had not to hide its real purpose under a carefully worded paragraph in theatrical programmes or on " dodgers " or hand-bills that had an existence of a moment before they were swept out into the street, and which, as they were not sent through mails, were not worthy the notice of the federal government.

It was not so very long ago that it requires any effort to remember it. It is only a few years since the lottery held its drawings freely and with much pomp and circumstance in the Charles Theatre, and Generals Beauregard and Early presided at these ceremonies, selling the names they had made glorious in a lost cause to help a cause which was, for the lottery people at least, distinctly a winning one. For in those days the state lottery cleared above all expenses seven million dollars a year, and Generals Beauregard and Early drew incomes from it much larger than the government paid to the judges of the Supreme Court and the members of the cabinet who finally declared against the company and drove it into exile.

There had been many efforts made to kill it

in the past, and the state lottery was called "the national disgrace" and "the modern slavery," and Louisiana was spoken of as a blot on the map of our country, as was Utah when polygamy flourished within her boundaries and defied the laws of the federal government. The final rally against the lottery occurred in 1890, when the lease of the company expired, and the directors applied to the legislature for a renewal. At that time it was paying out but very little and taking in fabulous sums; how much it really made will probably never be told, but its gains were probably no more exaggerated by its enemies than was the amount of its expenses by the company itself. Its outlay for advertising, for instance, which must have been one of its chief expenses, was only forty thousand dollars a year, which is a little more than a firm of soap manufacturers pay for their advertising for the same length of time; and it is rather discouraging to remember that for a share of this bribe every newspaper in the city of New Orleans and in the State of Louisiana, with a few notable exceptions, became an organ of the lottery, and said nothing concerning it but what was good. To this sum may be added the salaries of its officers, the money paid out in prizes, the cost of printing and mailing the tickets, and the sum of forty thousand dollars paid annually to the State of Louisiana. This tribute was considered as quite sufficient when the lottery was first start, ed, and while it struggled for ten years to make a living; but in 1890, when its continued existence was threatened, the company found it could very well afford to offer the state not forty thousand, but a million dollars a year, which gives a faint idea of what its net earnings must have been. As a matter of fact, in those palmy times when there were daily drawings, the lottery received on some days as many as eighteen to twenty thousand letters, with orders for tickets enclosed which averaged five dollars a letter.

It was Postmaster - general Wanamaker who put a stop to all this by refusing to allow any printed matter concerning the lottery to pass outside of the State of Louisiana, which decision, when it came, proved to be the order of exile to the greatest gambling concern of modern times.

The lottery, of course, fought this decision in the courts, and the case was appealed to the Supreme Court of the United States, and was upheld, and from that time no letter addressed to the lottery in this country, or known to contain matter referring to the lottery, and no newspaper advertising it, can pass through the mails. This ruling was known before the vote on the renewal of the lease came up in the Legislature of Louisiana, and the lottery people say that, knowing that they could not, under these new

restrictions, afford to pay the sum of one million
dollars a year, they ceased their efforts to pass
the bill granting a renewal of their lease, and let
it go without a fight. This may or may not be
true, but in any event the bill did not pass, and
the greatest lottery of all times was without a
place in which to spin its wheel, without a charter
or a home, and was cut off from the most obvious means of communication with its hundreds
of thousands of supporters. But though it was
excommunicated, outlawed, and exiled, it was
not beaten; it still retained agents all over the
country, and it still held its customers, who were
only waiting to throw their money into its lap,
and still hoping that the next drawing would
bring the grand prize.

For some long time the lottery was driven
about from pillar to post, and knocked eagerly
here and there for admittance, seeking a home
and resting-place. It was not at first successful.
The first rebuff came from Mexico, where it had
proposed to move its plant, but the Mexican
government was greedy, and wanted too large a
sum for itself, or, what is more likely, did not
want so well-organized a rival to threaten the
earnings of its own national lottery. Then the
republics of Colombia and Nicaragua were each
tempted with the honor of giving a name to the
new company, but each declined that distinction,
and so it finally came begging to Honduras, the

least advanced of all of the Central American republics, and the most heavily burdened with debt.

Honduras agreed to receive the exile, and to give it her name and protection for the sum of

THE EXILED LOTTERY BUILDING

twenty thousand dollars a year and twenty per cent. of its gross earnings. It would seem that this to a country that has not paid the interest

4

on her national debt for twelve years was a very
advantageous bargain ; but as four presidents
and as many revolutions and governments have
appeared and disappeared in the two years in
which the lottery people have received their
charter in Honduras, the benefit of the arrange-
ment to them has not been an obvious one,
and it was not until two years ago that the first
drawing of the lottery was held at Puerto Cortez.
The company celebrated this occasion with a
pitiful imitation of its former pomp and ceremony, and there was much feasting and speech-
making, and a special train was run from the interior to bring important natives to the ceremonies.   But the train fell off the track four times,
and was just a day late in consequence.   The
young man who had charge of the train told me
this, and he also added that he did not believe
in lotteries.

During these two years, when representatives
of the company were taking rides of nine days
each to the capital to overcome the objections of
the new presidents who had sprung into office
while these same representatives had been making their return trip to the coast, others were
seeking a foothold for the company in the United
States.   The need of this was obvious and im-
perative.   The necessity which had been forced
upon them of holding the drawings out of this
country, and of giving up the old name and

trade-mark, was serious enough, though it had been partially overcome. It did not matter where they spun their wheel; but if the company expected to live, there must be some place where it could receive its mail and distribute its tickets other than the hot little Honduranian port, locked against all comers by quarantine for six months of the year, and only to be reached during the other six by a mail that arrives once every eight days.

The lottery could not entirely overcome this difficulty, of course, but through the aid of the express companies of this country it was able to effect a substitute, and through this cumbersome and expensive method of transportation its managers endeavored to carry on the business which in the days when the post-office helped them had brought them in twenty thousand letters in twenty-four hours. They selected for their base of operations in the United States the port of Tampa, in the State of Florida—that refuge of prize-fighters and home of unhappy Englishmen who have invested in the swamp-lands there, under the delusion that they were buying town sites and orange plantations, and which masquerades as a winter resort with a thermometer that not infrequently falls below freezing. So Tampa became their home ; and though the legislature of that state proved incorruptible, so the lottery people themselves tell me, there was at least an understanding between them and those in authority that the express company was not to be disturbed, and that no other lottery was to have a footing in Florida for many years to come.

If Puerto Cortez proved interesting when it was only a name on a theatre programme, you may understand to what importance it grew when it could not be found on the map of any steamship company in New York, and when no paper of that city advertised dates of sailing to that port. For the first time Low's Exchange failed me and asked for time, and the ubiquitous Cook & Sons threw up their hands, and offered in desperation and as a substitute a comfortable trip to upper Burmah or to Mozambique, protesting that Central America was beyond even their finding out. Even the Maritime Exchange confessed to a much more intimate knowledge of the west coast of China than of the little group of republics which lies only a three or four days' journey from the city of New Orleans. So I was forced to haunt the shipping-offices of Bowling Green for days together, and convinced myself while so engaged that that is the only way properly to pursue the study of geography, and I advise every one to try it, and submit the idea respectfully to instructors of youth. For you will find that by the time you have interviewed fifty shipping-clerks, and learned from them where they can set you down and pick you

up and exchange you to a fruit-vessel or coasting steamer, you will have obtained an idea of
foreign ports and distances which can never be
gathered from flat maps or little revolving globes.
I finally discovered that there was a line running
from New York and another from New Orleans,
the fastest steamer of which latter line, as I
learned afterwards, was subsidized by the lottery
people.   They use it every month to take their
representatives and clerks to Puerto Cortez, when,
after they have held the monthly drawing, they
steam back again to New Orleans or Tampa,
carrying with them the list of winning numbers
and the prizes.

It was in the boat of this latter line that we
finally awoke one morning to find her anchored
in the harbor of Puerto Cortez.

The harbor is a very large one and a very safe
one.   It is encircled by mountains on the sea-
side, and by almost impenetrable swamps and
jungles on the other.   Close around the waters
of the bay are bunches and rows of the cocoanut
palm, and a village of mud huts covered with
thatch.   There is also a tin custom-house, which
includes the railroad-office and a *comandancia*,
and this and the jail or barracks of rotting whitewashed boards, and the half-dozen houses of one
story belonging to consuls and shipping agents,
are the only other frame buildings in the place
save one.   That is a large mansion with broad

verandas, painted in colors, and set in a carefully designed garden of rare plants and manaca palms. Two poles are planted in the garden, one flying the blue-and-white flag of Honduras, the other with the stripes and stars of the United States. This is the home of the exiled lottery. It is the most pretentious building and the cleanest in the whole republic of Honduras, from the Caribbean Sea to the Pacific slope.

I confess that I was foolish enough to regard this house of magnificent exterior, as I viewed it from the wharf, as seriously as a general observes the ramparts and defences of the enemy before making his advance. I had taken a nine days' journey with the single purpose of seeing and getting at the truth concerning this particular building, and whether I was now to be viewed with suspicion and treated as an intruder, whether my object would be guessed at once and I should be forced to wait on the beach for the next steamer, or whether I would be received with kindness which came from ignorance of my intentions, I could not tell. And while I considered, a black Jamaica negro decided my movements for me. There was a hotel, he answered, doubtfully, but he thought it would be better, if Mr. Barross would let me in, to try for a room in the Lottery Building.

"Mr. Barross sometimes takes boarders," he said, "and the Lottery Building is a fine house,

sir—finest house this side Mexico city." He
added, encouragingly, that he spoke English
"very good," and that he had been in London.

Sitting on the wide porch of the Lottery Building was a dark-faced, distinguished-looking little
man, a creole apparently, with white hair and
white goatee. He rose and bowed as I came up
through the garden and inquired of him if he
was the manager of the lottery, Mr. Barross, and
if he could give me food and shelter. The gentleman answered that he was Mr. Barross, and
that he could and would do as I asked, and
appealed with hospitable warmth to a tall, handsome woman, with beautiful white hair, to support him in his invitation. Mrs. Barross assent-
ed kindly, and directed her servants to place a
rocking-chair in the shade, and requested me to
be seated in it; luncheon, she assured me, would
be ready in a half-hour, and she hoped that the
voyage south had been a pleasant one.

And so within five minutes after arriving in
the mysterious harbor of Puerto Cortez I found
myself at home under the roof of the outlawed
lottery, and being particularly well treated by
its representative, and feeling particularly uncomfortable in consequence. I was heartily
sorry that I had not gone to the hotel. And so,
after I had been in my room, I took pains to
ascertain exactly what my position in the house
might be, and whether or not, apart from the

courtesy of Mr. Barross and his wife, for which
no one could make return, I was on the same
free footing that I would have been in a hotel.
I was assured that I was regarded as a transient
boarder, and that I was a patron rather than a
guest ; but as I did not yet feel at ease, I took
courage, and explained to Mr. Barross that I
was not a coffee-planter or a capitalist looking
for a concession from the government, but that I
was in Honduras to write of what I found there.
Mr. Barross answered that he knew already why
I was there from the New Orleans papers which
had arrived in the boat with me, and seemed
rather pleased than otherwise to have me about
the house.   This set my mind at rest, and though
it may not possibly be of the least interest to
the reader, it is of great importance to me that
the same reader should understand that all which
I write here of the lottery was told to me by
the lottery people themselves, with the full
knowledge that I was going to publish it.   And
later, when I had the pleasure of meeting Mr.
Duprez, the late editor of the *States*, in New
Orleans, and then in Tegucigalpa, as representative of the lottery, I warned him in the presence
of several of our friends to be careful, as I would
probably make use of all he told me.   To which
he agreed, and continued answering questions
for the rest of the evening.   I may also add that
I have taken care to verify the figures used here,

for the reason that the lottery people are at such an obvious disadvantage in not being allowed by law to reply to what is said of them, nor to correct any mistake in any statements that may be made to their disadvantage.

I had never visited a hotel or a country-house as curious as the one presided over by Mr. Barross. It was entirely original in its decoration, unique in its sources of entertainment, and its business office, unlike most business offices, possessed a peculiar fascination. The stationery for the use of the patrons, and on which I wrote to innocent friends in the North, bore the letter-head of the Honduras Lottery Company; the pictures on the walls were framed groups of lottery tickets purchased in the past by Mr. Barross, which had *not* drawn prizes; and the safe in which the guest might place his valuables contained a large canvas-bag sealed with red wax, and holding in prizes for the next drawing seventy-five thousand dollars.

Wherever you turned were evidences of the peculiar business that was being carried on under the roof that sheltered you, and outside in the garden stood another building, containing the printing-presses on which the lists of winning numbers were struck off before they were distributed broadcast about the world. But of more interest than all else was the long, sunshiny, empty room running the full length of the house,

in which, on a platform at one end, were two
immense wheels, one of glass and brass, and as
transparent as a bowl of goldfish, and the other
closely draped in a heavy canvas hood laced and
strapped around it, and holding sealed and locked
within its great bowels one hundred thousand
paper tickets in one hundred thousand rubber
tubes. In this atmosphere and with these surroundings my host and hostess lived their life of
quiet conventional comfort—a life full of the
lesser interests of every day, and lighted for others
by their most gracious and kindly courtesy and
hospitable good-will. When I sat at their table
I was always conscious of the great wheels, showing through the open door from the room beyond like skeletons in a closet; but it was not
so with my host, whose chief concern might be
that our glasses should be filled, nor with my
hostess, who presided at the head of the table—
which means more than sitting there—with that
dignity and charm which is peculiar to a Southern woman, and which made dining with ner an
affair of state, and not one of appetite.

I had come to see the working of a great gambling scheme, and I had anticipated that there
might be some difficulty put in the way of my
doing so; but if the lottery plant had been a
cider-press in an orchard I could not have been
more welcome to examine and to study it and
to take it to pieces. It was not so much that

they had nothing to conceal, or that now, while they are fighting for existence, they would rather risk being abused than not being mentioned at all. For they can fight abuse; they have had to do that for a long time. It is silence and oblivion that they fear now; the silence that means they are forgotten, that their arrogant glory has departed, that they are only a memory. They can fight those who fight them, but they cannot fight with people who, if they think of them at all, think of them as already dead and buried. It was neither of these reasons that gave me free admittance to the workings of the lottery; it was simply that to Mr. and Mrs. Barross the lottery was a religion; it was the greatest charitable organization of the age, and the purest philanthropist of modern times could not have more thoroughly believed in his good works than did Mrs. Barross believe that noble and generous benefits were being bestowed on mankind at every turn of the great wheel in her back parlor.

This showed itself in the admiration which she shares with her husband for the gentlemen of the company, and their coming once a month is an event of great moment to Mrs. Barross, who must find it dull sometimes, in spite of the great cool house, with its many rooms and broad porches, and gorgeous silk hangings over the beds, and the clean linen, and airy, sunlit dining-room. She is much more interested in telling the news that the gentlemen brought down with them when they last came than in the result of the drawing, and she recalls the compliments they paid her garden, but she cannot remember the number that drew the capital prize. It was interesting to find this big gambling scheme in the hands of two such simple, kindly people, and to see how commonplace it was to them, how much a matter of routine and of habit. They sang its praises if you wished to talk of it, but they were more deeply interested in the lesser affairs of their own household. And at one time we ceased discussing it to help try on the baby's new boots that had just arrived on the steamer, and patted them on the place where the heel should have been to drive them on the extremities of two waving fat legs. We all admired the tassels which hung from them, and which the baby tried to pull off and put in his mouth. They were bronze boots with black buttons, and the first the baby had ever worn, and the event filled the home of the exiled lottery with intense excitement.

In the cool of the afternoon Mr. Barross sat on the broad porch rocking himself in a big bent-wood chair and talked of the civil war, in which he had taken an active part, with that enthusiasm and detail with which only a Southerner speaks of it, not knowing that to this generation in the North it is history, and something of which one reads in books, and is not a topic of conversation of as fresh interest as the fall of Tammany or the Venezuela boundary dispute. And as we listened we watched Mrs. Barross moving about among her flowers with a sunshade above her white hair and holding her train in her hand, stopping to cut away a dead branch or to pluck a rose or to turn a bud away from the leaves so that it might feel the sun.

And inside, young Barross was going over the letters which had arrived with the morning's steamer, emptying out the money that came with them on the table, filing them away, and noting them as carefully and as methodically as a bank clerk, and sealing up in return the little green and yellow tickets that were to go out all over the world, and which had been paid for by clerks on small salaries, laboring-men of large families, idle good-for-nothings, visionaries, born gamblers and ne'er-do-wells, and that multitude of others of this world who want something for nothing, and who trust that a turn of luck will accomplish for them what they are too listless and faint-hearted and lazy ever to accomplish for themselves. It would be an excellent thing for each of these gamblers if he could look in at the great wheel at Puerto Cortez, and see just what one hundred thousand tickets look like, and what chance his one atom of a ticket has of forcing its way to the top of that great mass at the ex-

act moment that the capital prize rises to the
surface in the other wheel. He could have seen
it in the old days at the Charles Theatre, and he
is as free as is any one to see it to-day at Puerto
Cortez; but I should think it would be unfortunate for the lottery if any of its customers became too thorough a student of the doctrine of
chances.

The room in which the drawings are held is
about forty feet long, well lighted by many long,
wide windows, and with the stage upon which
the wheels stand blocking one end. It is unfur-
nished, except for the chairs and benches, upon
which the natives or any chance or intentional
visitors are welcome to sit and to watch the
drawing. The larger wheel, which holds, when
all the tickets are sold, the hopes of one hundred
thousand people, is about six feet in diameter,
with sides of heavy glass, bound together by a
wooden tire two feet wide. This tire or rim is
made of staves, formed like those of a hogshead,
and in it is a door a foot square. After the
tickets have been placed in their little rubber
jackets and shovelled into the wheel, this door is
locked with a padlock, and strips of paper are
pasted across it and sealed at each end, and so
it remains until the next drawing. One hundred
thousand tickets in rubber tubes an inch long
and a quarter of an inch wide take up a great
deal of space, and make such an appreciable

difference in the weight of the wheel that it requires the efforts of two men pulling on the handles at either side to even budge it. Another man and myself were quite satisfied when we had put our shoulders to it and had succeeded in turning it a foot or two. But it was interesting to watch the little black tubes with even that slow start go slipping and sliding down over the others, leaving the greater mass undisturbed and packed together at the bottom as a wave sweeps back the upper layer of pebbles on a beach. This wheel was manufactured by Jackson & Sharp, of Wilmington, Delaware. The other wheel is much smaller, and holds the prizes. It was made by John Robinson, of Baltimore.

Whenever there is a drawing, General W. L. Cabell, of Texas, and Colonel C. J. Villere, of Louisiana, who have taken the places of the late General Beauregard and of the late General Early, take their stand at different wheels, General Cabell at the large and Colonel Villere at the one holding the prizes. They open the doors which they had sealed up a month previous, and into each wheel a little Indian girl puts her hand and draws out a tube. The tube holding the ticket is handed to General Cabell, and the one holding the prize won is given to Colonel Villere, and they read the numbers aloud and the amount won six times, three times in Spanish and three times in English, on the principle probably of the man in the play who had only one line, and who spoke that twice, "so that the audience will know I am saying it."

The two tickets are then handed to young Barross, who fastens them together with a rubber band and throws them into a basket for further reference. Three clerks with duplicate books keep tally of the numbers and of the prizes won. The drawing begins generally at six in the morning and lasts until ten, and then, everybody having been made rich, the philanthropists and generals and colonels and Indian girls—and, let us hope, the men who turned the wheel—go in to breakfast.

So far as I could see, the drawings are conducted with fairness. But with only 3434 prizes and 100,000 tickets the chances are so infinitesimal and the advantage to the company so enormous that honesty in manipulating the wheel ceases to be a virtue, and becomes the lottery's only advertisement.

But what is most interesting about the lottery at present is not whether it is or it is not conducted fairly, but that it should exist at all; that its promoters should be willing to drag out such an existence at such a price and in so fallen a state. This becomes all the more remarkable because the men who control the lottery belong to a class which, as a rule, cares for the good opinion of its fellows, and is willing to sacrifice

THE IGUANAS OF HONDURAS

much to retain it. But the lottery people do not seem anxious for the good opinion of any one, and they have made such vast sums of money in the past, and they have made them so easily, that they cannot release their hold on the geese that are laying the golden eggs for them, even though they find themselves exiled and ex-communicated by their own countrymen. If they were thimble-riggers or confidence men in need of money their persistence would not appear so remarkable, but these gentlemen of the lottery are men of enormous wealth, their daughters are in what is called society in New Orleans and in New York, their sons are at the universities, and they themselves belong to those clubs most diffi-cult of access. One would think that they had reached that point when they could say "we are rich enough now, and we can afford to spend the remainder of our lives in making ourselves re-spectable." Becky Sharp is authority for the fact that it is easy to be respectable on as little as five hundred pounds a year, but these gentlemen, hav-ing many hundreds of thousands of pounds, are not even willing to make the effort. Two years ago, when, according to their own account, they were losing forty thousand dollars a month, which, after all, is only what they once cleared in a day, and when they were being driven out of one country after another, like the cholera or any other disease, it seems strange that it never occurred to them to stop fighting, and to get into a better business while there was yet time.

Even the keeper of a roulette wheel has too much self-respect to continue turning when there is only one man playing against the table, and in comparison with him the scramble of the lottery company after the Honduranian tin dollar, and the scant savings of servant-girls and of brakesmen and negro barbers in the United States, is to me the most curious feature of this once great enterprise.

What a contrast it makes with those other days, when the Charles Theatre was filled from boxes to gallery with the " flower of Southern chivalry and beauty," when the band played, and the major-generals proclaimed the result of the drawings. It is hard to take the lottery seriously, for the day when it was worthy of abuse has passed away. And, indeed, there are few men or measures so important as to deserve abuse, while there is no measure if it be for good so insignificant that it is not deserving the exertion of a good word or a line of praise and gratitude.

And the only emotion one can feel for the lottery now is the pity which you might have experienced for William M. Tweed when, as a fugitive from justice, he sat on the beach at Santiago de Cuba and watched a naked fisherman catch his breakfast for him beyond the first line of breakers, or that you might feel for Monte Carlo were it to be exiled to a fever-stricken island off the swampy coast of West Africa, or, to pay the lottery a very high compliment indeed, that which you give to that noble adventurer exiled to the Isle of Elba.

There was something almost pathetic to me in the sight of this great, arrogant gambling scheme, that had in its day brought the good name of a state into disrepute, that had boasted of the prices it paid for the honor of men, and that had robbed a whole nation willing to be robbed, spinning its wheel in a back room in a hot, half-barbarous country, and to an audience of gaping Indians and unwashed Honduranian generals. Sooner than fall as low as that it would seem to be better to fall altogether; to own that you are beaten, that the color has gone against you too often, and, like that honorable gambler and gentleman, Mr. John Oakhurst, who "struck a streak of bad luck about the middle of February, 1864," to put a pistol to your head, and go down as arrogantly and defiantly as you had lived.*

* Since this was written, Professor S. H. Woodbridge, of the Massachusetts Institute of Technology, has been successful in having a bill passed which hinders the lottery still further by closing to it apparently every avenue of advertisement and correspondence.

The lottery people in consequence are at present negotiating with the government of Venezuela, and have offered it fifty thousand dollars a year and a share of the earnings for its protection.

IN HONDURAS

I

TEGUCIGALPA is the odd name of the capital of the republic of Honduras, the least advanced of the republics of Central or South America. Somerset had learned that there were no means of getting to this capital from either the Pacific Ocean on one side or from the Caribbean Sea on the other except on muleback, and we argued that while there were many mining-camps and military outposts and ranches situated a nine days' ride from civilization, capitals at such a distance were rare, and for that reason might prove entertaining. Capitals at the mouths of great rivers and at the junction of many railway systems we knew, but a capital hidden away behind almost inaccessible mountains, like a monastery of the Greek Church, we had never seen. A door-mat in the front hall of a house is useful, and may even be ornamental, though it is

OUR NAVAL ATTACHÉ

never interesting; but if the door-mat be hidden away in the third-story back room it instantly
assumes an importance and a value which it
never could have attained in its proper sphere of
usefulness.

Our ideas as to the characteristics of Honduras were very vague, and it is possible that we
might never have seen Tegucigalpa had it not
been for Colonel Charles Jeffs, whom we found

apparently waiting for us at Puerto Cortez, and who, we still believe, had been stationed there by some guardian spirit to guide us in safety across the continent. Colonel Jeffs is a young American mining engineer from Minneapolis, and has lived in Honduras for the past eleven years. Some time ago he assisted Bogran, when that general was president, in one of the revolutions against him, and was made a colonel in consequence. So we called him our military attaché, and Griscom our naval attaché, because he was an officer of the Naval Brigade of Pennsylvania. Jeffs we found at Puerto Cortez. It was there that he first made himself known to us by telling our porters they had no right to rob us merely because we were gringos, and so saved us some dollars. He made us understand at the same time that it was as gringos, or foreigners, we were thereafter to be designated and disliked. We had no agreement with Jeffs, nor even what might be called an understanding. He had, as I have said, been intended by Providence to convey us across Honduras, and every one concerned in the outfit seemed to accept that act of kindly fate without question. We told him we were going to the capital, and were on pleasure bent, and he said he had business at the capital himself, and would like a few days' shooting on the way, so we asked him to come with us and act as guide, philosopher, and

friend, and he said, " The train starts at eight
to-morrow morning for San Pedro Sula, where I
will hire the mules." And so it was settled, and
we went off to get our things out of the custom-
house with a sense of perfect confidence in our
new acquaintance and of delightful freedom
from all responsibility. And though, perhaps, it
is not always best to put the entire charge of an
excursion through an unknown country into the
hands of the first kindly stranger whom you see
sitting on a hotel porch on landing, we found
that it worked admirably, and we depended on
our military attaché so completely that we never
pulled a cinch-strap or interviewed an ex-president without first asking his permission. I wish
every traveller as kindly a guide and as good a
friend.

The train to San Pedro Sula was made up of
a rusty engine and three little cars, with no
glass in the windows, and with seats too wide
for one person, and not at all large enough for
two. The natives made a great expedition of
this journey, and piled the cramped seats with
bananas and tortillas and old bottles filled with
drinking-water. We carried no luncheons ourselves, but we had the greater advantage of
them in that we were enjoying for the first time
the most beautiful stretch of tropical swamp
land and jungle that we came across during our
entire trip through Honduras. Sometimes the

train moved through tunnels of palms as straight
and as regular as the elms leading to an English
country-house, and again through jungles where
they grew in the most wonderful riot and dis-
order, so that their branches swept in through
the car-windows and brushed the cinders from
the roof. The jungle spread out within a few
feet of the track on either side, and we peered

OUR MILITARY ATTACHÉ

into an impenetrable net-work of vines and creepers and mammoth ferns and cacti and giant trees covered with orchids, and so tall that one could only see their tops by looking up at them from the rear platform.

The railroad journey from Puerto Cortez to San Pedro Sula lasts four hours, but the distance is only thirty-seven miles. This was, until a short time ago, when the line was extended by a New York company, the only thirty-seven miles of railroad track in Honduras, and as it has given to the country a foreign debt of $27,992,-850, the interest on which has not been paid since 1872, it would seem to be quite enough. About thirty years ago an interoceanic railroad was projected from Puerto Cortez to the Pacific coast, a distance of one hundred and forty-eight miles, but the railroad turned out to be a colossal swindle, and the government was left with this debt on its hands, an army of despoiled stockholders to satisfy, and only thirty-seven miles of bad road for itself. The road was to have been paid for at a certain rate per mile, and the men who mapped it out made it in consequence twice as long as it need to have been, and its curves and grades and turns would cause an honest engineer to weep with disapproval.

The grades are in some places very steep, and as the engine was not as young as it had been,

two negro boys and a box of sand were placed
on the cow-catcher, and whenever the necessity
of stopping the train was immediate, or when it
was going downhill too quickly, they would

A STRETCH OF CENTRAL-AMERICAN RAILWAY

lean forward and pour this sand on the rails.
As soon as Griscom and Somerset discovered
these assistant engineers they bribed them to
give up their places to them, and after the first

station we all sat for the remainder of the journey on the cow-catcher. It was a beautiful and
exhilarating ride, and suggested tobogganing, or
those thrilling little railroads on trestles at Co-
ney Island and at the fêtes around Paris. It was
even more interesting, because we could see each
rusty rail rise as the wheel touched its nearer
end as though it meant to fly up in our faces,
and when the wheel was too quick for it and
forced it down again, it contented itself by
spreading out half a foot or so to one side,
which was most alarming. And the interest rose
even higher at times when a stray steer would
appear on the rails at the end of the tunnel of
palms, as at the end of a telescope, and we saw
it growing rapidly larger and larger as the train
swept down upon it. It always lurched off to
one side before any one was killed, but not until
there had been much ringing of bells and blowing of whistles, and, on our part, some inward
debate as to whether we had better jump and
abandon the train to its fate, or die at our post
with our hands full of sand.

We lay idly at San Pedro Sula for four days,
while Jeffs hurried about collecting mules and
provisions. When we arrived we insisted on
setting forth that same evening, but the place
put its spell upon us gently but firmly, and
when we awoke on the third day and found we
were no nearer to starting than at the moment

THE THREE GRINGOS

of our arrival, Jeffs's perplexities began to be something of a bore, and we told him to put things off to the morrow, as did every one else.

San Pedro Sula lay in peaceful isolation in a sunny valley at the base of great mountains, and from the upper porch of our hotel, that had been built when the railroad was expected to continue on across the continent, we could see above the palms in the garden the clouds moving from one mountain-top to another, or lying packed like drifts of snow in the hollows between. We used to sit for hours on this porch in absolute idleness, watching Jeffs hurrying in and out below with infinite pity, while we listened to the palms rustling and whispering as they bent and courtesied before us, and saw the sunshine turn the mountains a light green, like dry moss, or leave half of them dark and sombre when a cloud passed in between. It was a clean, lazy little place of many clay huts, with gardens back of them filled with banana-palms and wide-reaching trees, which were one mass of brilliant crimson flowers. In the centre of the town was a grass-grown plaza where the barefooted and ragged boy-soldiers went through leisurely evolutions, and the mules and cows gazed at them from the other end.

Our hotel was leased by an American woman, who was making an unappreciated fight against dirt and insects, and the height of whose ambition was to get back to Brooklyn and take in light sewing and educate her two very young daughters. Her husband had died in the interior, and his portrait hung in the dining-room of the hotel. She used to talk about him while she was waiting at dinner, and of what a well-

read and able man he had been. She would
grow so interested in her stories that the dinner
would turn cold while she stood gazing at the
picture and shaking her head at it. We became
very much interested in the husband, and used
to look up over our shoulders at his portrait
with respectful attention, as though he were
present. His widow did not like Honduranians;
and though she might have made enough money
to take her home, had she consented to accept
them as boarders, she would only receive gringos
at her hotel, which she herself swept and scrubbed
when she was not cooking the dinner and making the beds. She had saved eight dollars of the
sum necessary to convey her and her children
home, and to educate them when they got there;
and as American travellers in Honduras are few,
and as most of them ask you for money to help
them to God's country, I am afraid her chance
of seeing the Brooklyn Bridge is very doubtful.
We contributed to her fund, and bought her a
bundle of lottery tickets, which we told her
were the means of making money easily; and I
should like to add that she won the grand prize,
and lived happily on Brooklyn Heights ever
after; but when we saw the list at Panama, her
numbers were not on it, and so, I fear, she is
still keeping the only clean hotel in Honduras, which is something more difficult to accomplish and a much more public-spirited

SETTING OUT FROM SAN PEDRO SULA

thing to do than to win a grand prize in a lottery.

We left San Pedro Sula on a Sunday morning, with a train of eleven mules; five to carry our luggage and the other six for ourselves, Jeffs, Charlwood, Somerset's servant, and Emilio, our chief moso, or muleteer. There were two other mosos, who walked the entire distance, and in bull-hide sandals at that, guarding and driving the pack-mules, and who were generally able to catch up with us an hour or so after we had halted for the night. I do not know which was the worst of the mosos, although Emilio seems to have been first choice with all of us. We agreed, after it was all over, that we did not so much regret not having killed them as that they could not know how frequently they had been near to sudden and awful death.

The people of Honduras, where all the travelling is done on mule or horse back, have a pretty custom of riding out to meet a friend when he is known to be coming to town, and of accompanying him when he departs. This latter ceremony always made me feel as though I were an undesirable citizen who was being conveyed outside of the city limits by a Vigilance Committee; but it is very well meant, and a man in Honduras measures his popularity by the number of friends who come forth to greet him on his arrival, or who speed him on his way when he

sets forth again.   We were accompanied out of
San Pedro Sula by the consular agent, the able
American manager of the thirty-seven miles
of railroad, and his youthful baggage-master, a
young gentleman whom I had formerly known
in the States.

Our escort left us at the end of a few miles,
at the foot of the mountains, and we began the
ascent alone.   From that time on until we
reached the Pacific Ocean we moved at the rate
of three miles an hour, or some nine leagues a
day, as distances are measured in Honduras, ten
hours being a day's journey.   Our mules were
not at all the animals that we know as mules in
the States, but rather overgrown donkeys or
burros, and not much stouter than those in the
streets of Cairo, whether it be the Street in
Cairo of Chicago, or the one that runs in front
of Shepheard's Hotel.   They were patient, plucky,
and wonderfully sure-footed little creatures, and
so careful of their own legs and necks that, after
the first few hours, we ceased to feel any anxiety
about our own, and left the entire charge of the
matter to them.

I think we were all a little startled at sight of
the trail we were expected to follow, but if we
were we did not say so—at least, not before Jeffs.
It led almost directly up the face of the mountain, along little ledges and pathways cut in
the solid rock, and at times was so slightly

THE HIGHLANDS OF HONDURAS

marked that we could not see it five yards ahead
of us. On that first day, during which the trail
was always leading upward, the mules did not
once put down any one of their four little feet
withe at first testing the spot upon which it was
to rest. This made our progress slow, but it
gave one a sense of security, which the angle
and attitude of the body of the man in front
did much to dissipate. I do not know the
name of the mountains over which we passed,
nor do I know the name of any mountain in
Honduras, except those which we named ourselves, for the reason that there is not much in
Honduras except mountains, and it would be as
difficult to give a name to each of her many
peaks as to christen every town site on a Western
prairie. When the greater part of all the earth
of a country stands on edge in the air, it would
be invidious to designate any one particular hill
or chain of hills. A Honduranian deputy once
crumpled up a page of letter-paper in his hand
and dropped it on the desk before him. " That,"
he said, " is an outline map of Honduras."

We rode in single file, with Jeffs in front,
followed by Somerset, with Griscom and myself
next, and Charlwood, the best and most faith-
ful of servants, bringing up the rear. The pack-
mules, as I have said, were two hours farther
back, and we could sometimes see them over
the edge of a precipice crawling along a thou-

sand feet below and behind us. It seemed an
unsociable way for friends to travel through a
strange country, and I supposed that in an hour
or so we would come
to a broader trail and
pull up abreast and
exchange tobacco
pouches and grow
better acquainted.
But we never came
to that broad trail
until we had trav-
elled sixteen days,
and had left Tegu-
cigalpa behind us,
and in the fore-
ground of all the
pictures I have in
my mind of Hondu-
ras there is always a
row of men's backs
and shoulders and
bobbing helmets dis-
appearing down a
slippery path of rock,
or rising above the
edge of a mountain
and outlined against
a blazing blue sky. We were generally near
enough to one another to talk if we spoke in

SOMERSET

a loud voice or turned in the saddle, though
sometimes we rode silently, and merely raised
an arm to point at a beautiful valley below or
at a strange bird on a tree, and kept it rigid
until the man behind said, "Yes, I see," when
it dropped, like a semaphore signal after the
train has passed.

Early in the afternoon of the day of our setting forth we saw for the last time the thatched
roofs of San Pedro Sula, like a bare spot in the
great green plain hundreds of feet below us,
and then we passed through the clouds we had
watched from the town itself, and bade the
eastern coast of Honduras a final farewell.

The trail we followed was so rough and uncer-
tain that at first I conceived a very poor opinion
of the Honduranians for not having improved it,
but as we continued scrambling upward I admired them for moving about at all under such
conditions. After all, we who had chosen to
take this road through curiosity had certainly no
right to complain of what was to the natives
their only means of communication with the Atlantic seaboard. It is interesting to think of a
country absolutely and entirely dependent on
such thoroughfares for every necessity of life.
For whether it be a postal card or a piano, or a
bale of cotton, or a box of matches, it must be
brought to Tegucigalpa on the back of a mule
or on the shoulders of a man, who must slip and

slide and scramble either over this trail or the one on the western coast.

Sometimes this high-road of commerce was cut through the living rock in steps as even and sharp as those in front of a brownstone house on Fifth Avenue, and so narrow that we had to draw up our knees to keep them from being scratched and cut on the rough walls of the passageway, and again it led through jungle so dense that if one wandered three yards from the trail he could not have found his way back again ; but this danger was not imminent, as no one could go that far from the trail without having first hacked and cut his way there.

It was not always so difficult; at times we came out into bare open spaces, and rode up the dry bed of a mountain stream, and felt the full force of the sun, or again it led along a ledge of rock two feet wide at the edge of a precipice, and we were fanned with cool, damp breaths from the pit a thousand feet below, where the sun had never penetrated, and where the moss and fern of centuries grew in a thick, dark tangle.

We stopped for our first meal at a bare place on the top of a mountain, where there were a half-dozen mud huts. Jeffs went from one to another of these and collected a few eggs, and hired a woman to cook them and to make us some coffee. We added tinned things and bread to this luncheon. which. as there were no benches.

A DRAWER OF WATER

we ate seated on the ground, kicking at the dogs and pigs and chickens, that snatched in a most familiar manner at the food in our hands. In Honduras there are so few hotels that travellers are entirely dependent for food and for a place in which to sleep upon the people who live along the trail, who are apparently quite hardened to having their homes invaded by strangers, and their larders levied upon at any hour of the day or night.

Even in the larger towns and so-called cities we slept in private houses, and on the solitary occasion when we were directed to a hotel we found a bare room with a pile of canvas cots heaped in one corner, to which we were told to help ourselves. There was a real hotel, and a very bad one, at the capital, where we fared much worse than we had often done in the interior; but with these two exceptions we were dependent for shelter during our entire trip across Honduras upon the people of the country. Sometimes they sent us to sleep in the town-hall, which was a large hut with a mud floor, and furnished with a blackboard and a row of benches, and sometimes with stocks for prisoners; for it served as a school or prison or hotel, according to the needs of the occasion.

We were equally dependent upon the natives for our food. We carried breakfast bacon and condensed milk and sardines and bread with us, and to these we were generally able to add, at least once a day, coffee and eggs and beans. The national bread is the tortilla. It is made of corn-meal, patted into the shape of a buckwheat cake between the palms of the hands, and then baked. They were generally given to us cold, in a huge pile, and were burned on both sides, but untouched by heat in the centre. The coffee was always excellent, as it should have been, for the Honduranian coffee is as fine as any grown in Central America, and we never had too much of it; but of eggs and black beans there was no end. The black-bean habit in Honduras is very general; they gave them to us three times a day, some-times cold and sometimes hot, sometimes with bacon and sometimes alone. They were fre-quently served to us in the shape of sandwiches between tortillas, and again in the form of pud-ding with chopped-up goat's meat. At first, and when they were served hot, I used to think them delicious. That seems very long ago now. When I was at Johnstown at the time of the flood, there was a soda cracker, with jam inside, which was served out to the correspondents in place of bread; and even now, if it became a question of my having to subsist on those crackers, and the black beans of Central America, or starve, I am sure I should starve, and by preference.

We were naturally embarrassed at first when we walked into strange huts; but the owners

seemed to take such invasions with apathy and
as a matter of course, and were neither glad to
see us when we came, nor relieved when we departed. They asked various prices for what they
gave us—about twice as much as they would
have asked a native for the same service; at least,
so Jeffs told us; but as our bill never amounted
to more than fifty cents apiece for supper, lodg-
ing, and a breakfast the next morning, they cannot be said to have robbed us. While the woman at the first place at which we stopped boiled
the eggs, her husband industriously whittled a
lot of sharp little sticks, which he distributed
among us, and the use of which we could not
imagine, until we were told we were expected
to spike holes in the eggs with them, and then
suck out the meat. We did not make a success
of this, and our prejudice against eating eggs
after that fashion was such that we were particular to ask to have them fried during the rest of
our trip. This was the only occasion when I saw
a Honduranian husband help his wife to work.

After our breakfast on the top of the mountain, we began its descent on the other side.
This was much harder on the mules than the
climbing had been, and they stepped even more
slowly, and so gave us many opportunities to
look out over the tops of trees and observe
with some misgivings the efforts of the man in
front to balance the mule by lying flat on its

hind-quarters. The temptation at such times to sit upright and see into what depths you were going next was very great. We struck a level trail about six in the evening, and the mules were so delighted at this that they started off of their own accord at a gallop, and were further encouraged by our calling them by the names of different Spanish generals. This inspired them to such a degree that we had to change their names to Bob Ingersoll or Senator Hill, or others to the same effect, at which they grew discouraged and drooped perceptibly.

We slept that night at a ranch called La Pieta, belonging to Dr. Miguel Pazo, where we experimented for the first time with our hammocks, and tried to grow accustomed to going to bed under the eyes of a large household of Indian maidens, mosos, and cowboys. There are men who will tell you that they like to sleep in a hammock, just as there are men who will tell you that they like the sea best when it is rough, and that they are happiest when the ship is throwing them against the sides and superstructure, and when they cannot sit still without bracing their legs against tables and stanchions. I always want to ask such men if they would prefer land in a state of perpetual earthquake, or in its normal condition of steadiness, and I have always been delighted to hear sea-captains declare themselves best pleased with a level keel, and the chance it gives them to go about their work without having to hang on to hand-rails. And I had a feeling of equal satisfaction when I saw as many sailors as could find room sleeping on the hard deck of a man-of-war at Colon, in preference to suspending themselves in hammocks, which were swinging empty over their heads. The hammock keeps a man at an angle of forty-five degrees, with the weight of both his legs and his body on the base of the spinal column, which gets no rest in consequence.

The hammock is, however, almost universally used in Honduras, and is a necessity there on account of the insects and ants and other beasts that climb up the legs of cots and inhabit the land. But the cots of bull-hide stretched on ropes are, in spite of the insects, greatly to be preferred; they are at least flat, and one can lie on them without having his legs three feet higher than his head. Their manufacture is very simple. When a steer is killed its hide is pegged out on the ground, and left where the dogs can eat what flesh still adheres to it; and when it has been cleaned after this fashion and the sun has dried it, ropes of rawhide are run through its edges, and it is bound to a wooden frame with the hairy side up. It makes a cool, hard bed. In the poorer huts the hides are given to the children at night, and spread directly on the earth floor. During the day the same hides are
7

used to hold the coffee, which is piled high upon them and placed in the sun to dry.

We left La Pieta early the next morning, in the bright sunlight, but instead of climbing laboriously into the sombre mountains of the day before, we trotted briskly along a level path between sunny fields and delicate plants, and trees with a pale-green foliage, and covered with the most beautiful white-and-purple flowers. There were hundreds of doves in the air, and in the bushes many birds of brilliant blue-and-black or orange-and-scarlet plumage, and one of more sober colors with two long white tail-feathers and a white crest, like a macaw that had turned Quaker. None of these showed the least inclination to disturb himself as we approached. An hour after our setting forth we plunged into a forest of manacca-palms, through which we rode the rest of the morning. This was the most beautiful and wonderful experience of our journey. The manacca-palm differs from the cocoanut or royal palm in that its branches seem to rise directly from the earth, and not to sprout, as do the others, from the top of a tall trunk. Each branch has a single stem, and the leaf spreads and falls from either side of this, cut into even blades, like a giant fern.

There is a plant that looks like the manacca-palm at home which you see in flower-pots in the corners of drawing-rooms at weddings, and conse-

NATIVE METHOD OF DRYING COFFEE

quently when we saw the real manacca-palm the effect was curious. It did not seem as though they were monster specimens of these little plants in the States, but as though we had grown smaller. We felt dwarfed, as though we had come across a rose-bush as large as a tree. The branches of these palms were sixty feet high, and occasionally six feet broad, and bent and swayed and interlaced in the most graceful and exquisite confusion. Every blade trembled in the air, and for hours we heard no other sound save their perpetual murmur and rustle. Not even the hoofs of our mules gave a sound, for they trod on the dead leaves of centuries. The palms made a natural archway for us, and the leaves hung like a portière across the path, and you would see the man riding in front raise his arm and push the long blades to either side, and disappear as they fell again into place behind him. It was like a scene on the tropical island of a pantomime, where every thing is exaggerated both in size and in beauty. It made you think of a giant aquarium or conservatory which had been long neglected.

At every hundred yards or so there were giant trees with smooth gray trunks, as even and regular as marble, and with roots like flying-buttresses, a foot in thickness, and reaching from ten to fifteen feet up from the ground. If these flanges had been covered over, a man on muleback could have taken refuge between them.

Some of the trunks of these trees were covered
with intricate lace-work of a parasite which
twisted in and out, and which looked as though
thousands of snakes were crawling over the
white surface of the tree; they were so much
like snakes that one passed beneath them with
an uneasy shrug. Hundreds of orchids clung to
the branches of the trees, and from these stouter
limbs to the more pliable branches of the palms
below white-faced monkeys sprang and swung
from tree to tree, running along the branches
until they bent with the weight like a trout-rod,
and sprang upright again with a sweep and rush
as the monkeys leaped off chattering into the
depths of the forest. We rode through this
enchanted wilderness of wavering sunlight and
damp, green shadows for the greater part of the
day, and came out finally into a broad, open
plain, cut up by little bubbling streams, flashing
brilliantly in the sun. It was like an awakening
from a strange and beautiful nightmare.

In the early part of the afternoon we arrived
at another one of the farm-houses belonging to
young Dr. Pazo, and at which he and his brother
happened to be stopping. We had ridden out
of our way there in the hopes of obtaining a few
days' shooting, and the place seemed to promise
much sport. The Chamelicon River, filled with
fish and alligators, ran within fifty yards of the
house; and great forests, in which there were

IN A CENTRAL-AMERICAN FOREST

bear and deer and wild-pig, stretched around it and beyond it on every side. The house itself was like almost every other native hut in Honduras. They are all built very much alike, with no attempt at ornamentation within, or landscape-gardening without, although nature has furnished the most beautiful of plants and trees close on every side for just such a purpose. The walls of a Honduranian hut are made of mud packed round a skeleton of interwoven rods; the floor is of the naked earth, and the roof is thatched with the branches of palms. After the house is finished, all of the green stuff growing around and about it is cleared away for fifty yards or so, leaving an open place of bare and barren mud. This is not decorative, but it helps in some measure to keep the insects which cling to every green thing away from the house. A kitchen of similarly interlaced rods and twigs, but without the clay, and covered with just such layers of palm leaves, stands on the bare place near the house, or leans against one side of it. This is where the tortillas are patted and baked, and the rice and beans are boiled, and the raw meat of an occasional goat or pig is hung to dry and smoke over the fire. The oven in the kitchen is made of baked clay, and you seldom see any cooking utensils or dishes that have not been manufactured from the trees near the house or the earth beneath it. The water for drinking and cooking is kept in round jars of red clay, which stand in rings of twisted twigs to keep them upright, and the drinking-vessels are the halves of gourds, and the ladles are whole gourds, with the branch on which they grew still adhering to them, to serve as a handle.

The furnishing of the house shows the same dependence upon nature; the beds are either grass hammocks or the rawhide that I have described, and there are no chairs and few benches, the people preferring apparently to eat sitting on their haunches to taking the trouble necessary to make a chair. Everything they eat, of which there is very little variety, grows just beyond the cleared place around the hut, and can be had at the cost of the little energy necessary to bring it in-doors. When a kid or a pig or a steer is killed, the owner goes out to the nearest peak and blows a blast on a cow's horn, and those within hearing who wish fresh meat hurry across the mountain to purchase it. As there is no ice from one end of Honduras to the other, meat has to be eaten the day it is killed.

This is not the life of the Honduranians who live in the large towns or so-called cities, where there are varying approaches to the comfort of civilized countries, but of the country people with whom we had chiefly to do. It is as near an approach to the condition of primitive man as one can find on this continent.

But bare and poor as are the houses, which are bare not because the people are poor, but because they are indolent, there is almost invariably some corner of the hut set aside and ornamented as an altar, or some part of the wall covered with pictures of a religious meaning. When they have no table, the people use a shelf or the stump of a tree upon which to place emblematic figures, which are almost always china dolls, with no original religious significance, but which they have dressed in little scraps of tinsel and silk, and which they have surrounded with sardine-tins and empty bottles and pictures from the lids of cigar-boxes. Everything that has color is cherished, and every traveller who passes adds unconsciously to their stock of ornaments in the wrappings of the boxes which he casts away behind him. Sometimes the pictures they use for ornamentation are not half so odd as the fact that they ever should have reached such a wilderness. We were frequently startled by the sight of colored lithographs of theatrical stars, advertising the fact that they were playing under the direction of such and such a manager, and patent-medicine advertisements and wood-cuts from illustrated papers, some of them twenty and thirty years old, which were pinned to the mud walls and reverenced as gravely as though they had been pictures of the Holy Family by a Raphael or a Murillo.

In one hut we found a life-size colored litho-graph of a woman whom, it so happened, we all knew, which was being used to advertise a sewing-machine. We were so pleased at meeting a fa-miliar face so far from home that we bowed to it very politely, and took off our hats, at which the woman of the house, mistaking our deference, placed it over the altar, fearing that she had been entertaining an angel unawares.

The house of Dr. Pazo, where we were most hospitably entertained, was similar to those that I have described. It was not his home, but what we would call a hunting-box or a ranch. While we were at luncheon he told a boy to see if there were any alligators in sight, in exactly the same tone with which he might have told a servant to find out if the lawn-tennis net were in place. The boy returned to say that there were five within a hundred yards of the house. So, after we had as usual patiently waited for Griscom to finish his coffee, we went out on the bank and fired at the unhappy alligators for the remainder of the afternoon. It did not seem to hurt them very much, and certainly did us a great deal of good. To kill an alligator it is necessary to hit it back of the fore-leg, or to break its spine where it joins the tail; and as it floats with only its eyes and a half-inch of its nose exposed, it is difficult to reach either of these vital spots. When the alligator is on a bank, and you at-

tempt to crawl up on it along the opposite bank,
the birds make such a noise, either on its account or on their own, that it takes alarm, and
rolls over into the water with an abruptness you
would hardly expect from so large a body.

On our second day at Dr. Pazo's ranch we
divided into two parties, and scoured the wilderness for ten miles around after game. One party
was armed with shot - guns, and brought back
macaws of wonderful plumage, wild turkeys, and
quail in abundance; the others, scorning anything but big game, carried rifles, and, as a result, returned as they set forth, only with fewer
cartridges. It was most unfortunate that the
only thing worth shooting came to me. It was
a wild-cat with a long tail, who patiently waited
for us in an open place with a calm and curious
expression of countenance. I think I was more
surprised than he was, and even after I had
thrown up the ground under his white belly he
stopped and turned again to look at me in a
hurt and reproachful manner before he bounded
gracefully out of sight into the underbrush. We
also saw a small bear, but he escaped in the
same manner, without waiting to be fired upon,
and as we had no dogs to send after him, we
gave up looking for more, and went back to pot
at alligators. There were some excellent hunting - dogs on the ranch, but the Pazo brothers
had killed a steer the night we arrived, and had

given most of it to the dogs, so that in the
morning they were naturally in no mood for
hunting.

There was an old grandfather of an alligator
whom Somerset and I had repeatedly disturbed
in his slumbers.   He liked to take his siestas on
a little island entirely surrounded by rapids, and
we used to shoot at him from the opposite bank
of the river.   He was about thirteen feet long,
and the agility with which he would flop over
into the calm little bay, which stretched out from
the point on which he slept, was as remarkable
as it was disappointing.   He was still asleep at
his old stand when we returned from our unsuc-
cessful shooting tour, so we decided to swim the
rapids and crawl up on him across his little island
and attack him from the flank and rear.   It reminded me somewhat of the taking of Lungten-
pen on a small scale.   On that occasion, if I
remember correctly, the raw recruits were uni-
formed only in Martinis and cartridge-belts; but
we decided to carry our boots as well, because
the alligator's island was covered with sharp
stones and briers, and the sand was very hot, and,
moreover, we had but vague ideas about the customs of alligators, and were not sure as to
whether he might not chase us.   We thought
we would look very silly running around a little
island pursued by a long crocodile and treading
on sharp hot stones in our bare feet.

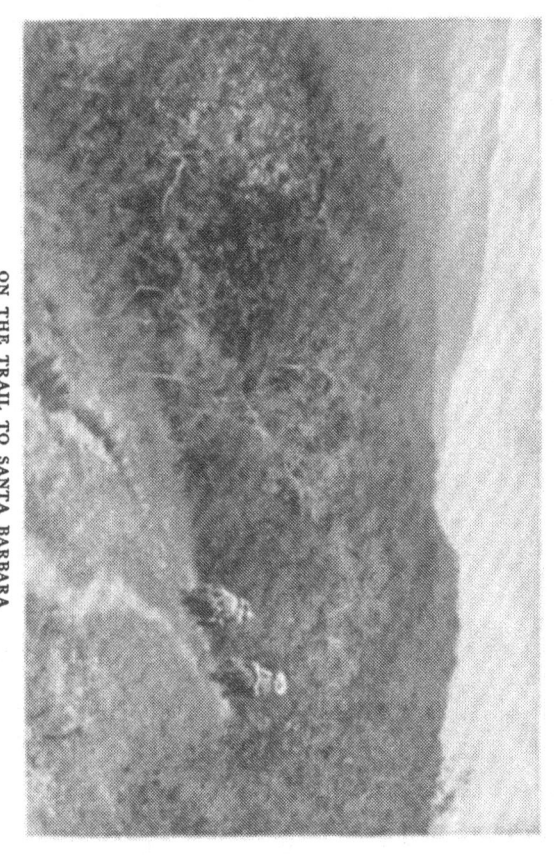

ON THE TRAIL TO SANTA BARBARA

So each of us took his boots in one hand and a repeating-rifle in the other, and with his money-belt firmly wrapped around his neck, plunged into the rapids and started to ford the river. They were exceedingly swift rapids, and made you feel as though you were swinging round a sharp corner on a cable-car with no strap by which to take hold. The only times I could stop at all was when I jammed my feet in between two stones at the bed of the river, and was so held in a vise, while the rest of my body swayed about in the current and my boots scooped up the water. When I wanted to go farther I would stick my toes between two more rocks, and so gradually worked my way across, but I could see nothing of Somerset, and decided that he had been drowned, and went off to avenge him on the alligator. It took me some time to get my bruised and bleeding toes into the wet boots, during which time I kept continually looking over my shoulder to see if the alligator were going to make a land attack, and surprise me instead of my surprising him. I knew he was very near me, for the island smelled as strongly of musk as a cigar-shop smells of tobacco; but when I crawled up on him he was still on his point of sand, and sound asleep. I had a very good chance at seventy yards, but I was greedy, and wanted to come closer, and as I was crawling along, gathering thorns and briers by the way, I

8

startled about fifty birds, and the alligator flopped over again, and left nothing behind him but a few tracks on the land and a muddy streak in the water. It was a great deal of trouble for a very little of alligator; but I was more or less consoled on my return to find that Somerset was still alive, and seated on the same bank from which we had both started, though at a point fifty yards farther down-stream. He was engaged in counting out damp Bank - of - England notes on his bare knee, and blowing occasional blasts down the barrel of his rifle, which had dragged him and itself to the bottom of the river before the current tossed them both back on the shore.

The two days of rest at the ranch of Dr. Pazo had an enervating effect upon our mules, and they moved along so slowly on the day following that we had to feel our way through the night for several hours before we came to the hut where we were to sleep. Griscom and I had lost ourselves on the mountain-side, and did not overtake the others until long after they had settled themselves in the compound. They had been too tired when they reached it to do anything more after falling off their mules, and we found them stretched on the ground in the light of a couple of fluttering pine torches, with cameras and saddle-bags and carbines scattered recklessly about, and the mules walking over them in the

A HALT AT TRINIDAD

darkness. A fire in the oven shone through the chinks in the kitchen wall, and showed the woman of the house stirring something in a caldron with one hand and holding her sleeping child on her hip with the other, while the daughters moved in and out of the shadow, carrying jars on their heads and bundles of fodder for the animals. It looked like a gypsy encampment. We sent Emilio back with a bunch of pine torches to find the pack-mules, and we could see his lighted torch blazing far up the trail that we had just descended, and lighting the rocks and trees on either side of him.

There was only room for one of us to sleep inside the hut that night, and as Griscom had a cold, that privilege was given to him; but it availed him little, for when he seated himself on the edge of the bull-hide cot and began to pull off his boots, five ghostly feminine figures sat upright in their hammocks and studied his preparations with the most innocent but embarrassing curiosity. So, after waiting some little time for them to go to sleep again, he gave up any thought of making himself more comfortable, and slept in his boots and spurs.

We passed through the pretty village of Trinidad early the next morning, and arrived at nightfall at the larger town of Santa Barbara, where the sound of our mules' hoofs pattering over the paved streets and the smell of smoking street lamps came to us with as much of a shock as does the sight of land after a week at sea. Santa Barbara, in spite of its pavements, was not a great metropolis, and, owing to its isolation, the advent of five strangers was so much of an event that the children of the town followed us, cheering and jeering as though we were a circus procession; they blocked the house in which we took refuge, on every side, so that the native policemen had to be stationed at our windows to wave them away. On the following morning we called to pay our respects on General Louis Bogran, who has been President of Honduras for eight years and an exile for two. He died a few months after our visit. He was a very handsome man, with a fine presence, and with great dignity of manner, and he gave us an audience exactly as though he were a dethroned monarch and we loyal subjects come to pay him homage in his loneliness. I asked him what he regarded as the best work of his administration, and after thinking awhile he answered, "Peace for eight years," which was rather happy, when you consider that in the three years since he had left office there have been four presidents and two long and serious revolutions, and when we were in the capital the people seemed to think it was about time to begin on another.

We left Santa Barbara early the next morning, and rode over a few more mountains to the town of Seguaca, where the village priest was holding a festival, and where the natives for many miles around had gathered in consequence.

GENERAL LOUIS BOGRAN

There did not seem to be much of interest going on when we arrived, for the people of the town and the visitors within her gates deserted the booths and followed us in a long procession down the single street, and invaded the house where we lunched.

Our host on this occasion set a table for us in the centre of his largest room, and the population moved in through the doors and windows, and seated themselves cross-legged in rows ten and fifteen deep on the earth floor at our feet, and regarded us gravely and in absolute silence. Those who could not find standing-room inside stood on the window-sills and blocked the door-ways, and the women were given places of honor on tables and beds. It was somewhat embarrassing, and we felt as though we ought to offer something more unusual than the mere exercise of eating in order to justify such interest; so we attempted various parlor tricks, without appearing to notice the presence of an audience, and pretended to swallow the eggs whole, and made knives and forks disappear in the air, and drew silver dollars from the legs of the table, continuing our luncheon in the meantime in a self-possessed and polite manner, as though such eccentricities were our hourly habit. We could see the audience, out of the corner of our eyes, leaning forward with their eyes and mouths wide open, and were so encouraged that we called up some of the boys and drew watches and dollars out of their heads, after which they retired into corners and ransacked their scantily clad persons for more. It was rather an ex-

OUR PACK-TRAIN AT SANTA BARBARA

pensive exhibition, for when we set forth again they all laid claim to the dollars of which they considered they had been robbed.

The men of the place, according to their courteous custom, followed us out of the town for a few miles, and then we all shook hands and exchanged cigars and cigarettes, and separated with many compliments and expressions of high esteem.

The trail from Seguaca to our next resting-place led through pine forests and over layers of pine-needles that had been accumulating for years. It was a very warm, dry afternoon, and the air was filled with the odor of the pines, and when we came to one of the many mountain streams we disobeyed Jeffs and stopped to bathe in it, and let it carry us down the side of the mountain with the speed of a toboggan. We had been told that bathing at any time was extreme-ly dangerous in Honduras, and especially so in the afternoon ; but we always bathed in the afternoon, and looked forward to the half-hour spent in one of these roaring rapids as the best part of the day. Of all our recollections of Honduras, they are certainly the pleasantest. The water was almost icily cold, and fell with a rush and a heavy downpour in little water-falls, or between great crevices in the solid rocks, leaping and bubbling and flashing in the sun, or else sweeping in swift eddies in the com-

pass of deep, shadowy pools. We used to im-
prison ourselves between two rocks and let a fall
of water strike us from the distance of several
feet on our head and shoulders, or tear past and
around us, so that in five minutes the soreness
and stiffness of the day's ride were rubbed out
of us as completely as though we had been
massaged at a Turkish bath, and the fact that
we were always bruised and black and blue when
we came out could not break us of this habit.
It was probably because we were new to the
country that we suffered no great harm; for
Jeffs, who was an old inhabitant, and who had
joined us in this particular stream for the first
time, came out looking twenty years older, and
in an hour his teeth were chattering with chills
or clinched with fever, and his pulse was jumping at one hundred and three. We were then
exactly six days' hard riding from any civilized
place, and though we gave him quinine and
whiskey and put him into his hammock as soon
as we reached a hut, the evening is not a cheerful one to remember. It would not have been
a cheerful evening under any circumstances, for
we shared the hut with the largest and most
varied collection of human beings, animals, and
insects that I have ever seen gathered into so
small a place.

I took an account of stock before I turned in,
and found that there were three dogs, eleven

cats, seven children, five men, not including five
of us, three women, and a dozen chickens, all
sleeping, or trying to sleep, in the same room,
under the one roof. And when I gave up at-
tempting to sleep and wandered out into the
night, I stepped on the pigs, and startled three
or four calves that had been sleeping under the
porch and that lunged up out of the darkness.
We were always asking Jeffs why we slept in
such places, instead of swinging our hammocks
under the trees and camping out decently and
in order, and his answer was that while there
were insects enough in-doors, they were virtually
an extinct species when compared to the number one would meet in the open air.

I have camped in our West, where all you
need is a blanket to lie upon and another to
wrap around you, and a saddle for a pillow, and
where, with a smouldering fire at your feet, you
can sleep without thought of insects. But there
is nothing green that grows in Honduras that is
not saturated and alive with bugs, and all manner of things that creep and crawl and sting and
bite. It transcends mere discomfort; it is an
absolute curse to the country, and to every one
in it, and it would be as absurd to write of Honduras without dwelling on the insects, as of the
west coast of Africa without speaking of the
fever. You cannot sit on the grass or on a fallen
tree, or walk under an upright one or through

the bushes, without hundreds of some sort of animal or other attaching themselves to your clothing or to your person. And if you get down from your mule to take a shot at something in the bushes and walk but twenty feet into them, you have to be beaten with brushes and rods when you come out again as vigorously as though you were a dusty carpet. There will be sometimes as many as a hundred insects under one leaf; and after they have once laid their claws upon you, your life is a mockery, and you feel at night as though you were sleeping in a bed with red pepper. The mules have even a harder time of it; for, as if they did not suffer enough in the day, they are in constant danger at night from vampires, which fasten themselves to the neck and suck out the blood, leaving them so weak that often when we came to saddle them in the morning they would stagger and almost fall. Sometimes the side of their head and shoulders would be wet with their own blood. I never heard of a vampire attacking a man in that country, but the fact that they are in the air does not make one sleep any the sounder.

In the morning after our night with the varied collection of men and animals we put back again to the direct trail to Tegucigalpa, from which place we were still distant a seven days' ride.

II

WE swung our hammocks on the sixth night out in the municipal building of Tabla Ve; but there was little sleep. Towards morning the night turned bitterly cold, and the dampness rose from the earthen floor of the hut like a breath from the open door of a refrigerator, and kept us shivering in spite of sweaters and rubber blankets. Above, the moon and stars shone brilliantly in a clear sky, but down in the valley in which the village lay, a mist as thick as the white smoke of a locomotive rose out of the ground to the level of the house-tops, and hid Tabla Ve as completely as though it were at the bottom of a lake. The dogs of the village moved through the mist, howling dismally, and meeting to fight with a sudden sharp tumult of yells that made us start up in our hammocks and stare at each other sleepily, while Jeffs rambled on, muttering and moaning in his fever. It was not a pleasant night, and we rode up the mountain-side out of the mist the next morning unrefreshed, but satisfied to be once more in the sunlight. They had told us at Tabla Ve that there was to be a bull-baiting that same afternoon at the village of

Seguatepec, fifteen miles over the mountain, where a priest was holding a church festival. So we left Jeffs to push along with the mozos, and by riding as fast as the mules could go, we reached Seguatepec by four in the afternoon.

A VILLAGE IN THE INTERIOR

It was a bright, clean town, sitting pertly on the flat top of a hill that fell away from it evenly on every side. It had a little church and a little plaza, and the church was so vastly superior to every other house in the place—as was the case in every village through which we passed—as to make one suppose that it had been built by one race of people and the houses by another. The plaza was shut in on two of its sides by a barrier seven rails high, held together by ox-hide ropes. This barrier, with the houses fronting the plaza on its two other sides, formed the arena in which the bull was to be set at liberty. All of the windows and a few of the doors of the houses were barred, and the open places between were filled up by ramparts of logs. There was no grand-stand, but every one contributed a bench or a table from his own house, and the women seated themselves on these, while the men and boys perched on the upper rail of the barricade. The occasion was a memorable one, and all the houses were hung with strips of colored linen, and the women wore their brilliant silk shawls, and a band of fifteen boys, none of whom could have been over sixteen years of age, played a weird overture to the desperate business of the afternoon.

It was a somewhat primitive and informal bull-fight, and it began with their lassoing the bull by his horns and hoofs, and dragging him head first against the barricade. With a dozen men pulling on the lariat around the horns from the outside of the ring, and two more twisting his tail on the inside, he was at such an uncomfortable disadvantage that it was easy for them to

9

harness him in a net-work of lariats, and for a bold rider to seat himself on his back. The bold rider wore spurs on his bare feet, and, with his toes stuck in the ropes around the bull's body, he grasped the same ropes with one hand, and with the other hand behind him held on to the bull's tail as a man holds the tiller of a boat. When the man felt himself firmly fixed, and the bull had been poked into a very bad temper with spears and sharp sticks, the lariat around his horns was cut, and he started up and off on a frantic gallop, bucking as vigorously as a Texas pony, and trying to gore the man clinging to his back with backward tosses of his horns.

There was no regular toreador, and any one who desired to sacrifice himself to make a Sagua-tepecan holiday was at liberty to do so; and as a half-dozen men so sought distinction, and as the bull charged at anything on two legs, the excitement was intense. He moved very quickly for so huge an animal in spite of his heavy handicap, and, with the exception of one man with a red flag and a spirit of daring not entirely due to natural causes, no one cared to go very near him. So he pawed up and down the ring, tossing and bucking and making himself as disagreeable to the man on his back as he possibly could. It struck me that it would be a distinctly sporting act to photograph a bull while he was charging head on at the photographer, and it occurred to

Somerset and Griscom at about the same time
that it would be pleasant to confront a very mad
bull while he was careering about with a man
twisting his tail. So we all dropped into the
arena at about the same moment, from different
sides, and as we were gringos, our appearance
was hailed with laughter and yells of encourage-
ment. The gentleman on the bull seemed to be
able to control him more or less by twisting his
tail to one side or the other, and as soon as he
heard the shouts that welcomed us he endeavored
to direct the bull's entire attention to my two
young friends. Griscom and Somerset are six
feet high, even without riding-boots and pith
helmets, and with them they were so conspicuous that the bull was properly incensed, and
made them hurl themselves over the barricade
in such haste that they struck the ground on the
other side at about the same instant that he
butted the rails, and with about the same amount
of force.

Shrieks and yells of delight rose from the
natives at this delightful spectacle, and it was
generally understood that we had been engaged
to perform in our odd costumes for their special
amusement, and the village priest attained gen-
uine popularity for this novel feature. The bull-
baiting continued for some time, and as I kept
the camera in my own hands, there is no docu-
mentary evidence to show that any one ran away

but Griscom and Somerset. Friendly doors were opened to us by those natives whose houses formed part of the arena, and it was amusing to see the toreadors popping in and out of them, like the little man and woman on the barometer who come out when it rains and go in when the sun shines, and *vice versa*.

On those frequent occasions when the bull charged the barricade, the entire line of men and boys on its topmost rail would go over backward, and disappear completely until the disappointed bull had charged madly off in another direction. Once he knocked half of a mud-house away in his efforts to follow a man through a doorway, and again a window-sill, over which a toreador had dived head first like a harlequin in a pantomime, caved in under the force of his attack. Fresh bulls followed the first, and the boy musicians maddened them still further by the most hideous noises, which only ceased when the bulls charged the fence upon which the musicians sat, and which they vacated precipitately, each taking up the tune where he had left off when his feet struck the ground. There was a grand ball that night, to which we did not go, but we lay awake listening to the fifteen boy musicians until two in the morning. It was an odd, eyrie sort of music, in which the pipings of the reed instruments predominated. But it was very beautiful, and very much like the music of the

Hungarian gypsies in making little thrills chase up and down over one's nervous system.

The next morning Jeffs had shaken off his fever, and, once more reunited, we trotted on over heavily wooded hills, where we found no water until late in the afternoon, when we came upon a broad stream, and surprised a number of young girls in bathing, who retreated leisurely as we came clattering down to the ford. Bathing in mid-stream is a popular amusement in Honduras, and is conducted without any false sense of modesty; and judging from the number of times we came upon women so engaged, it seems to be the chief occupation of their day.

That night we slept in Comyagua, the second largest city in the republic. It was originally selected as the site for a capital, and situated accordingly at exactly even distances from the Pacific Ocean and the Caribbean Sea. We found it a dull and desolate place of many one-story houses, with iron-barred windows, and a great, bare, dusty plaza, faced by a huge cathedral. Commerce seemed to have passed it by, and the sixty thousand inhabitants who occupied it in the days of the Spaniards have dwindled down to ten. The place is as completely cut off from civilization as an island in the Pacific Ocean. The plain upon which Comyagua stands stretches for many miles, and the nature of the stones and pebbles on its surface would seem to show that it was once the bottom of a great lake. Now its round pebbles and sandy soil make it a valley of burning heat, into which the sun beats without the intervening shadows of trees or mountains to save the traveller from the fierceness of its rays.

We rode over thirty miles of it, and found that part of the plain which we traversed after our night's rest at the capital the most trying ten miles of our trip. We rode out into it in the rear of a long funeral procession, in which the men and boys walked bareheaded and barefooted in the burning sand. They were marching to a burial-ground out in the plain, and they were carrying the coffin on their shoulders, and bearing before it a life-sized figure of the Virgin and many flaring candles that burned yellow in the glaring sunlight.

From Comyagua the trail led for many miles through heavy sand, in which nothing seemed to grow but gigantic cacti of a sickly light green that twisted themselves in jointed angles fifteen to twenty feet in the air above us, and century-plants with flowers of a vivid yellow, and tall, leafless bushes bristling with thorns. The mountains lay on either side, and formed the valley through which we rode, two dark-green barriers against a blazing sky, but for miles before and behind us there was nothing to rest the eye from the glare of the sand. The atmosphere was

without a particle of moisture, and the trail
quivered and swam in the heat; if you placed
your hand on the leather pommel of your saddle
it burned the flesh like a plate of hot brass, and
ten minutes after we had dipped our helmets in
water they were baked as dry as when they had
first come from the shop. The rays of the sun
seemed to beat up at you from below as well
as from above, and we gasped and panted as we
rode, dodging and ducking our heads as though
the sun was something alive and active that
struck at us as we passed by. If you dared to
look up at the sky its brilliancy blinded you as
though some one had flashed a mirror in your
eyes.

We lunched at a village of ten huts planted
defiantly in the open plain, and as little protected from the sun as a row of bricks in a brick-
yard, but by lying between two of them we found
a draught of hot air and shade, and so rested for
an hour. Our trail after that led over a mile or
two of red hematite ore, which suggested a ride
in a rolling-mill with the roof taken away, and
with the sun beating into the four walls, and the
air filled with iron-dust. Two hours later we
came to a cañon of white chalk, in which the
government had cut stepping-places for the hoofs
of the mules. The white glare in this valley was
absolutely blinding, and the atmosphere was that
of a lime-kiln. We showed several colors after

this ride, with layers of sand and clay, and particles of red ore and powdering of white chalk over
all; but by five o'clock we reached the mountains once more, and found a cool stream dash-
ing into little water-falls and shaded by great
trees, where the air was scented by the odor of
pine-needles and the damp, spongy breath of
moss and fern.

We were now within two days of Tegucigalpa, and the sense of nearness to civilization and
the knowledge that the greater part of our journey was at an end made us forget the discom-
forts and hardships which we had endured without the consolation of excitement that comes
with danger, or the comforting thought that we
were accomplishing anything in the meantime.
We had been complaining of this during the
day to Jeffs, and saying that had we gone to the
coast of East Africa we could not have been
more uncomfortable nor run greater risks from
fever, but that there we would have met with
big game, and we would have visited the most
picturesque instead of the least interesting of all
countries.

These complaints inspired Jeffs to play a trick
upon us, which was meant in a kindly spirit, and
by which he intended to furnish us with a moment's excitement, and to make us believe that
we had been in touch with danger. There are
occasional brigands in Central America, and their

BRIDGE CONNECTING TEGUCIGALPA WITH ITS SUBURB

favorite hunting-ground in Honduras is within a few miles of Tegucigalpa, along the trail from the eastern coast over which we were then passing. We had been warned of these men, and it occurred to Jeffs that as we complained of lack of excitement in our trip, it would be a thoughtful kindness to turn brigand and hold us up upon our march. So he left us still bathing at the water-fall, and telling us that he would push on to engage quarters for the night, rode some distance ahead and secreted himself behind a huge rock on one side of a narrow cañon. He first placed his coat on a bush beside him, and his hat on another bush, so as to make it appear that there were several men with him. His idea was that when he challenged us we would see the dim figures in the moonlight and remember the brigands, and that we were in their stalking-ground, and get out of their clutches as quickly as possible, well satisfied that we had at last met with a real adventure.

We reached his ambuscade about seven. Somerset was riding in advance, reciting " The Walrus and the Carpenter," while we were correcting him when he went wrong, and gazing unconcernedly and happily at the cool moonlight as it came through the trees, when we were suddenly startled by a yell and an order to halt, in Spanish, and a rapid fusillade of pistol-shots. We could distinguish nothing but what was appar-

ently the figures of three men crouching on the
hill-side and the flashes of their revolvers, so we
all fell off our mules and began banging away at
them with our rifles, while the mules scampered
off down the mountain. This was not as Jeffs
had planned it, and he had to rearrange matters
very rapidly. Bullets were cutting away twigs
all over the hill-side and splashing on the rock
behind which he was now lying, and though he
might have known we could not hit him, he was
afraid of a stray bullet. So he yelled at us in
English, and called us by name, until we finally
discovered we had been grossly deceived and imposed upon, and that our adventure was a very
unsatisfactory practical joke for all concerned. It
took us a long time to round up the mules, and
we reached our sleeping-place in grim silence,
and with our desire for danger still unsatisfied.

The last leagues that separated us the next
morning from Tegucigalpa seemed, of course,
the longest in the entire journey. And so great
was our desire to reach the capital before nightfall that we left the broader trail and scrambled
down the side of the last mountain, dragging our
mules after us, and slipping and sliding in dust and
rolling stones to the tops of our boots. The city
did not look inviting as we viewed it from above.
It lay in a bare, dreary plain, surrounded by five
hills that rose straight into the air, and that
seemed to have been placed there for the special

BIRD'S-EYE VIEW OF TEGUCIGALPA

purpose of revolutionists, in order that they might the more exactly drop shot into the town at their feet. The hills were bare of verdure, and the landscape about the capital made each

THE BANK OF HONDURAS

of us think of the country about Jerusalem. As none of us had ever seen Jerusalem, we foregathered and argued why this should be so, and decided that it was on account of the round rocks lying apart from one another, and low, bushy trees, and the red soil, and the flat roofs of the houses.

The telegraph wire which extends across Honduras, swinging from trees and piercing long

stretches of palm and jungle, had warned the
foreign residents of the coming of Jeffs, and
some of them rode out to make us welcome.
Their greeting, and the sight of paved streets,
and the passing of a band of music and a guard
of soldiers in shoes and real uniform, seemed to
promise much entertainment and possible comfort.   But the hotel was a rude shock. We had
sent word that we were coming, and we had
looked forward eagerly to our first night in a
level bed under clean linen; but when we arrived
we were offered the choice of a room just vacated by a very ill man, who had left all of his med-
icines behind him, so that the place was unpleas-
antly suggestive of a hospital, or a very small
room, in which there were three cots, and a layer of dirt over all so thick that I wrote my name
with the finger of my riding-glove on the centre-
table.   The son of the proprietor saw this, and,
being a kindly person and well disposed, dipped
his arm in water and proceeded to rub it over
the top of the table, using his sleeve as a wash-
rag. So after that we gave up expecting anything pleasant, and were in consequence delight-
fully surprised when we came upon anything
that savored of civilization.

Tegucigalpa has an annex which lies on the
opposite side of the river, and which is to the
capital what Brooklyn is to New York.   The
river is not very wide nor very deep, and its

course is impeded by broad, flat rocks. The washer-women of the two towns stand beside these all day knee-deep in the eddies and beat the stones with their twisted clubs of linen, so that their echo sounds above the roar of the river like the banging of shutters in the wind or the reports of pistols. This is the only suggestion of energy that the town furnishes. The other inhabitants seem surfeited with leisure and irritable with boredom. There are long, dark, cool shops of general merchandise, and a great cathedral and a pretty plaza, where the band plays at night and people circle in two rings, one going to the right and one going to the left, and there is the government palace and a big penitentiary, a university and a cemetery. But there is no color nor ornamentation nor light nor life nor bustle nor laughter. You do not hear people talking and calling to one another across the narrow streets of the place by day or serenading by night. Every one seems to go to bed at nine o'clock, and after that hour the city is as silent as its great graveyard, except when the boy policemen mark the hour with their whistles or the street dogs meet to fight.

The most interesting thing about the capital is the fact to which I have already alluded, that everything in it and pertaining to it that was not dug from the ground or fashioned from trees was carried to it on the backs of mules.

10

The letter-boxes on the street corners had once been United States letter-boxes, and had later swung across the backs of donkeys. The gas-lamps and the iron railings of the parks, the few statues and busts in the public places, reached

STATUE OF MORAZAN

Tegucigalpa by the same means, and the great equestrian statue of Morazan the Liberator, in the plaza, was cast in Italy, and had been brought to Tegucigalpa in pieces before it was put together like a puzzle and placed in its pres-ent position to mark a glorious and victorious immortality. These things were not interesting in themselves, but it was interesting that they were there at all.

On the second day after our arrival the vice-president, Luis Bonilla, who bears the same last name but is no near relation to President Bonilla, took the oath of office, and we saw the ceremony with the barefooted public in the reception-room of the palace. The hall was hung with lace curtains and papered with imitation marble, and the walls were decorated with crayon portraits of Honduranian presidents. Bogran was not among them, nor was Morazan. The former was missing because it was due to him that young Bonilla had been counted out when he first ran for the presidency three years ago, when he was thirty-three years old, and the portrait of the Liberator was being reframed, because Bonilla's followers six months before had unintentionally shot holes through it when they were besieging the capital. The ceremony of swearing in the vice-president did not last long, and what impressed us most about it was the youth of the members of the cabinet and of the Supreme Court who delivered the oath of office. They belonged distinctly to the politician class as one sees it at home, and were young men of eloquent speech and elegant manners, in frock-coats and white ties. We came to know most of the president's followers later, and found them

hospitable to a degree, although they seemed
hardly old enough or serious enough to hold
place in the government of a republic, even so
small a one as Honduras. What was most ad-
mirable about each of them was that he had
fought and bled to obtain the office he held.
That is hardly a better reason for giving out
clerkships and cabinet portfolios than the reasons which obtain with us for distributing the
spoils of office, but you cannot help feeling more
respect for the man who has marched by the side
of his leader through swamps and through jungle,
who has starved on rice, who has slept in the
bushes, and fought with a musket in his hand in
open places, than for the fat and sleek gentlemen
who keep open bar at the headquarters of their
party organization, who organize marching clubs,
and who by promises or by cash secure a certain
amount of influence and a certain number of votes.

They risk nothing but their money, and if their
man fails to get in, their money is all they lose;
but the Central American politician has to show
the faith that is in him by going out on the
mountain-side and hacking his way to office with
a naked machete in his hand, and if *his* leader
fails, he loses his life, with his back to a church
wall, and looking into the eyes of a firing squad,
or he digs his own grave by the side of the road,
and stands at one end of it, covered with clay
and sweat, and with the fear of death upon him,

and takes his last look at the hot sun and the palms and the blue mountains, with the buzzards wheeling about him, and then shuts his eyes, and is toppled over into the grave, with a half-dozen bullets in his chest and stomach. That is what I should like to see happen to about half of our professional politicians at home. Then the other half might understand that holding a public office is a very serious business, and is not merely meant to furnish them with a livelihood and with places for their wives' relations.

I saw several churches and cathedrals in Honduras with a row of bullet-holes in the front wall, about as high from the ground as a man's chest, and an open grave by the road-side, which had been dug by the man who was to have occupied it. The sight gave us a vivid impression of the uncertainties of government in Central America. The man who dug this particular grave had been captured, with two companions, while they were hastening to rejoin their friends of the government party. His companions in misery were faint-hearted creatures, and thought it mattered but little, so long as they had to die, in what fashion they were buried. So they scooped out a few feet of earth with the tools their captors gave them, and stood up in the hollows they had made, and were shot back into them, dead; but the third man declared that he was not going to let his body lie so near the surface of the earth

that the mules could kick his bones and the
next heavy freshet wash them away. He accordingly dug leisurely and carefully to the depth
of six feet, smoothing the sides and sharpening
the corners, and while he was thus engaged at

GENERAL LOUIS BOGRAN, EX-PRESIDENT

the bottom of the hole he heard yells and shots
above him, and when he poked his head up over
the edge of the grave he saw his own troops running down the mountain-side, and his enemies
disappearing before them. He is still alive, and

frequently rides by the hole in the road-side on his way to the capital. The story illustrates the advisability of doing what every one has to do in this world, even up to the very last minute, in a thorough and painstaking manner.

There do not seem to be very many men killed in these revolutions, but the ruin they bring to the country while they last, and which continues after they are over, while the "outs" are getting up another revolution, is so serious that any sort of continued prosperity or progress is impossible. Native merchants will not order goods that may never reach them, and neither do the gringos care to make contracts with men who in six months may not only be out of office, but out of the country as well. Sometimes a revolution takes place, and half of the people of the country will not know of it until it has been put down or has succeeded; and again the revolution may spread to every boundary, and all the men at work on the high-roads and in the mines or on the plantations must stop work and turn to soldiering, and pack-mules are seized, the mail-carriers stopped, plantations are devastated, and forced loans are imposed upon those who live in cities, so that every one suffers more or less through every change of executive. During the last revolution Tegucigalpa was besieged for six months, and was not captured until most of the public buildings had been torn open by cannon

from the hills around the town, and the dwell-
ing-houses still show where bullets marked the
mud and plaster of the walls or buried themselves in the wood-work. The dining-room of
our hotel was ventilated by such openings, and
we used to amuse ourselves by tracing the course
of the bullets from the hole they had made at
one side of the room to their resting-place in the
other. The native Honduranian is not energetic,
and, except in the palace, there has been but
little effort made by the victors to cover up the
traces of their bombardment. Every one we met
had a different experience to relate, and pointed
out where he was sitting when a particular hole
appeared in the plaster before him, or at which
street corner a shell fell and burst at his feet.

It follows, of course, that a government which
is created by force of arms, and which holds itself in place by the same power of authority, cannot be a very just or a very liberal one, even if
its members are honest, and the choice of a ma-
jority of the people, and properly in office in
spite of the fact that they fought to get there,
and not on account of it. Bonilla was undoubtedly at one time elected President of Honduras,
although he did not gain the presidential chair
until after he had thrown his country into war
and had invaded it at the head of troops from
the rival republic of Nicaragua.

The Central-American cannot understand that

BARRACKS OF TEGUCIGALPA AFTER THE ATTACK OF THE REVOLUTIONISTS

when a bad man is elected to office legally it is better in the long-run that he should serve out his full term than that a better man should drive him out and defy the constitution. If he could be brought to comprehend that when the constitution says the president must serve four years that means four years, and not merely until some one is strong enough to overthrow him, it might make him more careful as to whom he elected to office in the first place. But the value of stability in government is something they cannot be made to understand. It is not in their power to see it, and the desire for change and revolution is born in the blood. They speak of a man as a "good revolutionist" just as we would speak of some one being a good pianist, or a good shot, or a good executive officer. It is a recognized calling, and the children grow up into fighters; and even those who have lived abroad, and who should have learned better, begin to plot and scheme as soon as they return to their old environment.

In each company of soldiers in Honduras there are two or three little boys in uniform who act as couriers and messengers, and who are able, on account of their slight figure, to penetrate where a man would be seen and shot. One of the officers in the revolution of 1894 told me he had sent six of these boys, one after another, with despatches across an open plain

which was being raked by the rifles of the enemy. And as each boy was killed as he crawled
through the sage-brush the other boys begged of
their colonel to let them be the next to go,
jumping up and down around him and snapping
their fingers like school-boys who want to at-
tract the attention of their teacher.

In the same revolution a young man of great
promise and many acquirements, who had just
returned from the States with two degrees from
Columbia College, and who should have lived to
turn his education to account in his own country, was killed with a rifle in his hand the third
day after his arrival from New York. In that
city he would probably have submitted cheerful-
ly to any imposition of the law, and would have
taken it quite as a matter of course had he been
arrested for playing golf on Sunday, or for riding
a bicycle at night without a lamp; but as soon
as this graduate of Columbia smelled the powder floating on his native air he loaded a rifle,
and sat out all day on the porch of his house
taking chance shots at the revolutionists on the
hill-side, until a chance shot ended him and his
brilliant career forever. The pity of it is that so
much good energy should be wasted in obtaining such poor results, for nothing better ever
seems to follow these revolutions. There is
only a new form of dictatorship, which varies
only in the extent of its revenge and in the pun-

ishments it metes out to its late opponents, but which must be, if it hopes to remain in power, a dictatorship and an autocracy.

The republics of Central America are republics in name only, and the movements of a

MORAZAN, THE LIBERATOR OF HONDURAS

stranger within the boundaries of Honduras are as closely watched as though he were a newspaper correspondent in Siberia. I often had to sign the names of our party twice in one day for the benefit of police and customs officers, and we never entered a hotel or boarded a steamer or disembarked from one that we were not carefully checked and receipted for exactly as though we were boxes of merchandise or registered letters. Even the natives cannot walk the street after nightfall without being challenged by sentries, and the collection of letters we received from alcaldes and comandantes and governors and presidents certifying to our being reputable citizens is large enough to paper the side of a wall. The only time in Central America when our privacy was absolutely unmolested, and when we felt as free to walk abroad as though we were on the streets of New York, was when we were under the protection of the hated monarchical institution of Great Britain at Belize, but never when we were in any of these disorganized military camps called free republics.

The Central - American citizen is no more fit for a republican form of government than he is for an arctic expedition, and what he needs is to have a protectorate established over him, either by the United States or by another power; it does not matter which, so long as it leaves the Nicaragua Canal in our hands. In the capital of Costa Rica there is a statue of the Republic in the form of a young woman standing with her foot on the neck of General Walker, the American filibuster. We had planned to go to the capital for the express purpose of tearing that statue down some night, or blowing it up; so it is perhaps just as well for us that we could not get there; but it would have been a very good thing for Costa Rica if Walker, or any other man of force, had put his foot on the neck of every republic in Central America and turned it to some account.

Away from the coasts, where there is fever, Central America is a wonderful country, rich and beautiful, and burdened with plenty, but its people make it a nuisance and an affront to other nations, and its parcel of independent little states, with the pomp of power and none of its dignity, are and will continue to be a constant danger to the peace which should exist between two great powers.

There is no more interesting question of the present day than that of what is to be done with the world's land which is lying unimproved; whether it shall go to the great power that is willing to turn it to account, or remain with its original owner, who fails to understand its value. The Central-Americans are like a gang of semibarbarians in a beautifully furnished house, of which they can understand neither its possibilities of comfort nor its use. They are the dogs in the manger among nations. Nature has given to their country great pasture-lands, wonderful forests of rare woods and fruits, treasures of silver and gold and iron, and soil rich enough to sup-

11

ply the world with coffee, and it only waits for
an honest effort to make it the natural highway
of traffic from every portion of the globe.   The
lakes of Nicaragua are ready to furnish a passageway which should save two months of sailing around the Horn, and only forty-eight miles of
swamp-land at Panama separate the two greatest
bodies of water on the earth's surface.   Nature
has done so much that there is little left for man
to do, but it will have to be some other man than
a native-born Central-American who is to do it.

We had our private audience with President
Bonilla in time, and found him a most courteous
and interesting young man.   He is only thirty-
six years of age, which probably makes him the
youngest president in the world, and he carries
on his watch-chain a bullet which was cut out of
his arm during the last revolution.   He showed
us over the palace, and pointed out where he
had shot holes in it, and entertained us most
hospitably.   The other members of the cabinet
were equally kind, making us many presents, and
offering Griscom a consul - generalship abroad,
and consulates to Somerset and myself, but we
said we would be ambassadors or nothing; so
they offered to make us generals in the next
revolution, and we accepted that responsible
position with alacrity, knowing that not even the
regiments to which we were accredited could
force us again into Honduras.

Before we departed the president paid us a very doubtful compliment in asking us to ride with him. We supposed it was well meant, but we still have secret misgivings that it was a plot to rid himself of us and of the vice-president at the same time. When his secretary came to tell us that Dr. Bonilla would be glad to have us ride with him at five that afternoon, I recalled the fact that all the horses I had seen in Honduras were but little larger than an ordinary donkey, and quite as depressed and spiritless. So I accepted with alacrity. The other two men, being cross-country riders, and entitled to wear the gold buttons of various hunt clubs on their waistcoats, accepted as a matter of course. But when we reached the palace we saw seven or eight horses in the patio, none under sixteen hands high, and each engaged in dragging two or three grooms about the yard, and swinging them clear of the brick tiles as easily as a sailor swings a lead. The president explained to us that these were a choice lot of six stallions which he had just imported from Chili, and that three of them had never worn a saddle before that morning.

He gave one of these to Griscom and another one to the vice-president, for reasons best known to himself, and the third to Somerset. Griscom's animal had an idea that it was better to go backward like a crab than to advance, so he

backed in circles around the courtyard, while
Somerset's horse seemed best to enjoy rearing
himself on his hind-legs, with the idea of rubbing
Somerset off against the wall; and the vice-
president's horse did everything that a horse can
do, and a great many things that I should not
have supposed a horse could do, had I not seen
it. I put my beast's nose into a corner of the
wall where he could not witness the circus per-
formance going on behind him, and I watched
the president's brute turning round and round
and round until it made me dizzy. We strangers confessed later that we were all thinking of
exactly the same thing, which was that, no matter how many of our bones were shattered, we
must not let these natives think they could ride
any better than any chance American or Englishman, and it was only a matter of national
pride that kept us in our saddles. The vice-
president's horse finally threw him into the doorway and rolled on him, and it required five of
his officers to pull the horse away and set him
on his feet again. The vice-president had not
left his saddle for an instant, and if he handles his men in the field as he handled that
horse, it is not surprising that he wins many
battles.

Not wishing to have us all killed, and seeing
that it was useless to attempt to kill the vice-
president in that way, Dr. Bonilla sent word to

the band to omit their customary salute, and so
we passed out in grateful silence between breath-
less rows of soldiers and musicians and several
hundreds of people who had never seen a life-
sized horse before. We rode at a slow pace, on
account of the vice-president's bruises, while the
president pointed out the different points from
which he had attacked the capital. He was not
accompanied by any guard on this ride, and informed us that he was the first president who
had dared go abroad without one. He seemed
to trust rather to the good-will of the *pueblo*, to
whom he plays, and to whom he bowed much
more frequently than to the people of the richer
class. It was amusing to see the more prominent
men of the place raise their hats to the president,
and the young girls in the suburbs nodding casu-
ally and without embarrassment to the man. Before he set out on his ride he stuck a gold-plated
revolver in his hip-pocket, which was to take the
place of the guard of honor of former presidents,
and to protect him in case of an attempt at assassination. It suggested that there are other
heads besides those that wear a crown which rest
uneasy.

It was a nervous ride, and Griscom's horse
added to the excitement by trying to back him
over a precipice, and he was only saved from
going down one thousand yards to the roofs of
the city below by several of the others dragging

at the horse's bridle. When, after an hour, we found ourselves once more within sight of the palace, we covertly smiled at one another, and are now content never to associate with presidents again unless we walk.

We left Tegucigalpa a few days later with a generous escort, including all the consuls, and José Guiteris, the assistant secretary of state, and nearly all of the foreign residents. We made such a formidable showing as we raced through the streets that it suggested an uprising, and we cried, "Viva Guiteris!" to make the people think there was a new revolution in his favor. We shouted with the most loyal enthusiasm, but it only served to make Guiteris extremely unhappy, and he occupied himself in considering how he could best explain to Bonilla that the demonstration was merely an expression of our idea of humor. Twelve miles out we all stopped and backed the mules up side by side, and everybody shook hands with everybody else, and there were many promises to write, and to forward all manner of things, and assurances of eternal remembrance and friendship, and then the Guiteris revolutionists galloped back, firing parting salutes with their revolvers, and we fell into line again with a nod of satisfaction at being once more on the road.*

* Guiteris died a few months after our visit.

We never expected any conveniences or comforts on the road, and so we were never disappointed, and were much happier and more contented in consequence than at the capital, where the name promised so much and the place furnished so little. We found that it was not the luxuries of life that we sighed after, but the mere conveniences—those things to which we had become so much accustomed that we never supposed there were places where they did not exist. A chair with a back, for example, was one of the things we most wanted. We had never imagined, until we went to Honduras, that chairs grew without backs; but after we had ridden ten hours, and were so tired that each man found himself easing his spinal column by leaning forward with his hands on the pommel of his saddle, we wanted something more than a three-legged stool when we alighted for the night.

Our ride to the Pacific coast was a repetition of the ride to the capital, except that, as there was a full moon, we slept in the middle of the day and rode later in the night. During this nocturnal journey we met many pilgrims going to the festivals. They were all mounted on mules, and seemed a very merry and jovial company. Sometimes there were as many as fifty in one party, and we came across them picnicking in the shade by day, or jogging along in the moonlight in a cloud of white dust, or a cloud of white foam as

they forded the broad river and their donkeys
splashed and slipped in the rapids. The nights
were very beautiful and cool, and the silence under the clear blue sky and white stars was like
the silence of the plains. The moon turned
the trail a pale white, and made the trees on
either side of it alive with shadows that seemed
to play hide-and-seek with us, and the stumps
and rocks moved and gesticulated with life,
until we drew up even with them, when they
were transformed once more into wood and
stone.

It was on the third day out from the capital,
while we were picking our way down the side of
a mountain, that Jeffs pointed to what looked
like a lake of silver lying between two great hills,
and we knew that we had crossed the continent,
and so raised our hats and saluted the Pacific
Ocean. A day later, after a long, rapid ride over
a level plain where the trail was so broad that we
could ride four abreast, we came to San Lorenzo,
a little cluster of huts at the edge of the ocean.
The settlement was still awake, for a mule train
of silver had just arrived from the San Rosario
mines, and the ruddy glare of pine knots was
flashing through the chinks in the bamboo walls
of the huts, and making yellow splashes of color
in the soft white light of the moon. We swung
ourselves out of the saddles for the last time, and
gave the little mules a farewell pat and many

ON THE WAY TO CORINTO

thanks, to which they made no response whatsoever.

Five hours later we left the continent for the island of Amapala, the chief seaport of the Pacific side of Honduras, and our ride was at an end. We left San Lorenzo at two in the morning, but we did not reach Amapala, although it was but fifteen miles out to sea, until four the next afternoon. We were passengers in a long, open boat, and slept stretched on our blankets at the bottom, while four natives pulled at long sweeps. There were eight cross-seats, and a man sat on every other one. A log of wood in which steps had been cut was bound to each empty seat, and it was up this that the rower walked, as though he meant to stand up on the seat to which it was tied, but he would always change his mind and sink back again, bracing his left leg on the seat and his right leg on the log, and dragging the oar through the water with the weight of his body as he sank backwards. I lay on the ribs of the boat below them and watched them through the night, rising and falling with a slight toss of the head as they sank back, and with their brown naked bodies outlined against the sky-line. They were so silent and their movements so regular that they seemed like statues cut in bronze. By ten the next morning they became so far animated as to say that they were tired and hungry, and would we allow them to rest on a little island that lay half a mile off our bow? We were very glad to rest ourselves, and to get out of the sun and the glare of the sea, and to stretch our cramped limbs; so we beached the boat in a little bay, and frightened off thousands of gulls, which rose screaming in the air, and which were apparently the only inhabitants.

The galley-slaves took sticks of driftwood and scattered over the rocks, turning back the seaweed with their hands, and hacking at the base of the rocks with their improvised hammers. We found that they were foraging for oysters; and as we had nothing but a tin of sardines and two biscuits among five of us, and had had nothing to eat for twenty-four hours, we followed their example, and chipped the oysters off with the butts of our revolvers, and found them cool and coppery, like English oysters, and most refreshing. It was such a lonely little island that we could quite imagine we were cast away upon it, and began to play we were Robinson Crusoe, and took off our boots and went in wading, paddling around in the water after mussels and crabs until we were chased to shore by a huge shark. Then every one went to sleep in the sand until late in the afternoon, when a breeze sprang up, and a boatman carried us out on his shoulders, and we dashed off gayly under full sail to the isle of Amapala, where we bade good-bye to Colonel Jeffs and to the Republic of Honduras.

We had crossed the continent at a point where it was but little broader than the distance from Boston to New York, a trip of five hours by train, but which had taken us twenty-two days.

AT CORINTO

EVERY now and again each of us, either through his own choice or by force of circumstance, drops out of step with the rest of the world, and retires from it into the isolation of a sick-room, or to the loneliness of the deck of an ocean steamer, and for some short time the world somehow manages to roll on without him.

He is like a man who falls out of line in a regiment to fasten his shoelace or to fill his canteen, and who hears over his shoulder the hurrying tramp of his comrades, who are leaving him farther and farther behind, so that he has to run briskly before he can catch up with them and take his proper place once more in the procession.

I shall always consider the ten days we spent at Corinto, on the Pacific side of Nicaragua, while we waited for the steamer to take us south to Panama, as so many days of non-existence,

as so much time given to the mere exercise of
living, when we were no more of this world than
are the prisoners in the salt-mines of Siberia, or
the keepers of light-houses scattered over sunny
seas, or the men who tend toll-gates on empty
country lanes. And so when I read in the newspapers last fall that three British ships of war
were anchored in the harbor of Corinto, with
their guns loaded to the muzzles with ultima-
tums and no one knows what else besides, and
that they meant to levy on the customs dues of
that sunny little village, it was as much of a shock
to me as it would be to the inhabitants of Sleepy
Hollow were they told that that particular spot
was wanted as a site for a World's Fair.

For no ships of any sort, certainly no ships of
war, ever came to Corinto while we occupied the
only balcony of its only hotel. Indeed, that was
why we were there, and had they come we would
have gone with them, no matter to what port
they were bound, even to the uttermost parts of
the earth.

We had come to Corinto from the little island
of Amapala, which lies seventy-five miles farther
up the coast, and which guards the only port
of entry to Honduras on the Pacific seaboard.
It is supposed to belong to the Republic of Honduras, but it is in reality the property of Rossner
Brothers, who sell everything from German machetes to German music-boxes, and who could,

PRINCIPAL HOTEL AND PRINCIPAL HOUSE AT CORINTO

if they wanted it, purchase the entire Republic of Honduras in the morning, and make a present of it to the Kaiser in the course of the afternoon. You have only to change the name of Rossner Brothers to the San Rosario Mining Company, to the Pacific Mail, to Errman Brothers, to the Panama Railroad Company, and you will identify the actual rulers of one or of several of the republics of Central America.

It is very well for President Zelaya, or Barrios, or Vasquez, or whatever his name may happen to be this month, to write to the New York

Herald and tell the people of the United States what the revolution in his country means. It does no harm; no one in the United States reads the letter, except the foreign editor who translates it, and no one in his own country ever sees it, but it makes him happy in thinking he is persuading some one that he governs in his own way. As a matter of fact he does not. His country, no matter what her name may be, is ruled by a firm of coffee-merchants in New York city, or by a German railroad company, or by a line of coasting steamers, or by a great trading-house, with headquarters in Berlin or London or Bordeaux. If the president wants money he borrows it from the trading-house; if he wants arms, or his soldiers need blankets, the trading-house supplies them. No one remembers now who was President of Peru when Henry Meiggs was alive, and to-day William L. Grace is a better name on letters of introduction to Chili and Peru than that of a secretary of state.

When we were in Nicaragua, one little English banking-house was fighting the minister of finance and the minister of foreign affairs and the president and the entire government, and while the notes issued by the bank were accepted at their face value, those of the government were taken only in the presence of a policeman or a soldier, who was there to see that you did take them. You find this condition of affairs all through

12

Central America, and you are not long in a republic before you learn which merchant or which
bank or which railroad company controls it, and
you soon grow to look upon a mule loaded with
boxes bearing the trade-mark of a certain busi-
ness-house with more respect than upon a soldier who wears the linen ribbon of the government.   For you know that at a word the soldier
will tear the ribbon from his straw sombrero and
replace it with another upon which is printed
"Viva Dr. Somebody Else," while the trade-
mark of the business - house will continue as
long as English and German merchandise is carried across the sea in ships.   And it will also
continue as long as Great Britain and Germany
and the United States are represented by consuls and consular agents who are at the same
time the partners of the leading business firms
in the seaport over which their consular juris-
diction extends.   For few Central-American republics are going to take away a consul's exe-
quatur as long as they owe him in his unofficial
capacity for a large loan of money; and the
merchant, on the other hand, knows that he is
not going to suffer from the imposition of a
forced loan, nor see his mules seized, as long as
the tin sign with the American eagle screaming
upon it is tacked above the brass business plate
of his warehouse.

There was a merchant in Tegucigalpa named

Santos Soto — he is there still, I believe — and about a year ago President Vasquez told him he needed a loan of ten thousand dollars to assist him in his struggle against Bonilla; and as Soto was making sixty thousand dollars a year in the country, he suggested that he had better lend it promptly. Soto refused, and was locked in the cartel, where it was explained to him that for every day he delayed in giving the money the amount demanded of him would be increased one thousand dollars. As he still refused, he was chained to an iron ball and led out to sweep the streets in front of his shop, which extends on both sides of the principal thoroughfare of the capital. He is an old man, and the sight of the chief merchant in Tegucigalpa sweeping up the dust in front of his own block of stores had a most salutary effect upon the other merchants, who promptly loaned the sums demanded of them, taking rebates on customs dues in exchange — with one exception. This merchant owned a jewelry store, and was at the same time the English consular agent. He did not sweep the streets, nor did he contribute to the forced loan. He values in consequence his tin sign, which is not worth much as a work of art, at about ten thousand dollars.

There is much that might be written of consular agents in Central America that would differ widely from the reports written by themselves and published by the State Department. The most interesting thing about them, to my mind, is the fact that none of them ever seem to represent a country which they have ever seen, and that they are always citizens of another country to which they are anxious to return. I find that after Americans, Germans make the best American consular agents, and Englishmen the best German consular agents, while French consular agents would be more useful to their countrymen if they could speak French as well as they do Spanish. Sometimes, as in the case of the consular agent at Corinto, you find a native of Italy representing both Great Britain and the United States. A whole comic opera could be written on the difficulties of a Nicaraguan acting as an English and American consul, with three British men-of-war in the harbor levying on the customs dues of his native land, and an American squadron hastening from Panama to see that their English cousins did not gather in a few islands by mistake.

If he called on the British admiral, and received his seven-gun salute, would it constitute a breach of international etiquette if he were rowed over to the American admiral and received seven guns from him; and as a native of Nicaragua could he see the customs dues, which comprise the government's chief source of revenue, going into the pockets of one country which he so proudly serves without complaining to the other country which he serves with equal satisfaction? Every now and then you come across a real American consul who was born in America, and who serves the United States with ability, dignity, and self-respect, so that you are glad you are both Americans. Of this class we found General Allen Thomas at La Guayra, who was later promoted and made United States minister at Caracas, Mr. Alger at Puerto Cortez, Mr. Little at Tegucigalpa, and Colonel Bird at Caracas.

We found that the firm of Rossner Brothers had in their employ the American and English consular agents, and these gentlemen endeared themselves to us by assisting at our escape from their island in an open boat. They did not tell us, however, that Fonseca Bay was one of the most treacherous stretches of water on the admiralty charts; but that was, probably, because they were merchants and not sailors.

Amapala was the hottest place I ever visited. It did not grow warm as the day wore on, but began briskly at sunrise by nailing the mercury at fever-heat, and continued boiling and broiling until ten at night. By one the next morning the roof over your head and the bed-linen beneath you had sufficiently cooled for you to sleep, and from that on until five there was a fair imitation of night.

There was but one cool spot in Amapala; it

was a point of land that the inhabitants had rather tactlessly selected as a dumping-ground for the refuse of the town, and which was only visited by pigs and buzzards. This point of land ran out into the bay, and there had once been an attempt made to turn it into a public park, of which nothing now remains but a statue to Morazan, the Liberator of Honduras. The statue stood on a pedestal of four broad steps, surrounded by an iron railing, the gates of which had fallen from their hinges, and lay scattered over the piles of dust and débris under which the park is buried. At each corner of the railing there were beautiful macaws which had once been painted in brilliant reds and greens and yellows, and which we tried to carry off one night, until we found that they also were made of iron. We would have preferred the statue of Morazan as a souvenir, but that we doubted its identity. Morazan was a smooth-faced man with a bushy head of hair, and this statue showed him with long side-whiskers and a bald head, and in the uniform of an English admiral. It was probably the rejected work of some English sculptor, and had been obtained, no doubt, at a moderate price, and as very few remember Morazan to-day it answers its purpose excellently well. We became very much attached to it, and used to burn incense to it in the form of many Honduranian cigars, which sell at two cents apiece.

When night came on, and the billiard-room had grown so hot that the cues slipped in our hands, and the tantalizing sight of an American ice-cooler, which had never held ice since it left San Francisco, had driven us out into the night, we would group ourselves at the base of this statue to Morazan, and throw rocks at the buzzards and pigs, and let the only breeze that dares to pass over Amapala bring our temperature down to normal. We should have plotted a revolution by rights, for the scene was set for such a purpose, and no one in the town accounted in any other way for our climbing the broken iron railing nightly, and remaining on the steps of the pedestal until two the next morning.

Amapala, I suppose, was used to heat, and could sleep with the thermometer at ninety, and did not mind the pigs or the buzzards, and if we did plot to convert Honduras into a monarchy and make Somerset king, no one heard us but the English edition of Morazan smiling blandly down upon us like a floor-walker at the Army and Navy Stores, with his hand on his heart and an occasional buzzard soaring like Poe's raven above his marble forehead. The moonlight turned him into a figure of snow, and the great palms above bent and waved and shivered unceasingly, and the sea beat on the rocks at our feet.

It was an interesting place of rendezvous, but

we tired of a town that grew cool only after midnight, and in which the fever stalked abroad by
day. So we chartered a small boat, and provi-
sioned it, and enlisted a crew of pirates, and set
sail one morning for Corinto, seventy-five miles
farther south. There was no steamer expected
at Corinto at any earlier date than at Amapala,
but in the nature of things one had to touch
there some time, and there was a legend to which
we had listened with doubt and longing to the
effect that at Corinto there was an ice-machine,
and though we found later that the ice-machines
always broke on the day we arrived in port,
we preferred the chance of finding Fonseca Bay
in a peaceful state to yellow-fever at Amapala.
It was an exciting voyage. I would now, being
more wise, choose the yellow-fever, but we did
not know any better then. There was no deck
to the boat, and it was not wide enough for one
to lie lengthwise from side to side, and too
crowded to permit of our stretching our bodies
fore and aft. So we rolled about on top of one
another, and were far too miserable to either
apologize or swear when we bumped into a man's
ribs or sat on his head.

We started with a very fine breeze dead astern,
and the boat leaped and plunged and rolled all
night, and we were hurled against the sides and
thumped by rolling trunks, and travelling-bags,
and gun-cases, and boxes of broken apollinaris

bottles. The stone-breaker in a quarry would
have soothed us in comparison. And when the
sun rose fully equipped at four in the morning
the wind died away absolutely, and we rose and
sank all day on the great swell of the Pacific
Ocean. The boat was painted a bright red inside and out, and the sun turned this open red
bowl into an oven of heat. It made even our
white flannels burn when they touched the skin
like a shirt of horse-hair. As far as we could
look on every side the ocean lay like a sea of
quicksilver, and the dome of the sky glittered
with heat. The red paint on the sides bubbled
and cracked, and even the native boatmen cow-
ered under the cross-seats with their elbows fold-
ed on their knees and their faces buried in their
arms; and we had not the heart to tell them to
use the oars, even if we had known how. At
noon the chief pirate crawled over the other
bodies and rigged up the sail so that it threw a
shadow over mine, and I lay under this awning
and read Barrie's *Lady Nicotine*, while the type
danced up and down in waving lines like the letters in a typewriter. I am sure it was only the
necessity which that book impressed upon me of
holding on to life until I could smoke the Arca-
dia mixture that kept me from dropping over-
board and being cremated in the ocean below.

We sighted the light-house of Corinto at last,
and hailed the white custom-house and the palms

and the blue cottages of the port with a feeble cheer.

The people came down to the shore and crowded around her bow as we beached her in front of the custom-house, and a man asked us anxiously in English, " What ship has been wrecked ?" And we explained that we were not survivors of a shipwreck, but of a possible conflagration, and wanted ice.

And then, when we fell over the side bruised and sleepy, and burning with thirst, and with everything still dancing before our eyes, they refused to give us ice until we grew cooler, and sent out in the meanwhile to the *comandancia* in search of some one who could identify us as escaped revolutionists. They took our guns away from us as a precaution, but they could have had half our kingdom for all we cared, for the wonderful legend proved true, and at last we got the ice in large, thick glasses, with ginger ale and lemon juice and apollinaris water trickling through it, and there was frost on the sides of the glasses, and a glimpse of still more ice wrapped up in smoking blankets in the refrigerator—ice that we had not tasted for many days of riding in the hot sun and through steaming swamp-lands, and which we had last seen treated with contempt and contumely, knocked about at the bow of a tug-boat in the North River, and tramped upon by many muddy feet on Fifth Avenue. None of us will ever touch ice hereafter without handling it with the same respect and consideration that we would show to a precious stone.

The busybodies of Corinto who had decided from the manner of our arrival that we had been forced to leave Honduras for the country's good, finally found a native who identified me as a filibuster he had met during the last revolution at Leon. As that was bringing it rather near home, Griscom went after Mr. Palaccio, the Italian who serves both England and the United States as consular agent. We showed him a rare collection of autographs of secretaries, ambassadors, and prime-ministers, and informed him that we intended taking four state-rooms on the steamer of the line he represented at that port. This convinced him of the necessity of keeping us out of jail until the boat arrived, and he satisfied the local authorities as to our respectability, and that we had better clothes in our trunks.

Corinto is the best harbor on the Pacific side of Nicaragua, but the town is not as large as the importance of the port would suggest. It consists of three blocks of two-story houses, facing the harbor fifty feet back from the water's edge, with a sandy street between each block of buildings. There are about a thousand inhabitants, and a foreign population which varies from five residents to a dozen transient visitors and stewards on steamer days. The natives are chiefly occupied in exporting coffee and receiving the imported goods for the interior, and the principal amusement of the foreign colony is bathing or playing billiards. It has a whist club of four members. The fifth foreign resident acts as a substitute in the event of any one of the four players chancing to have another engagement, but as there is no one with whom he could have an engagement, the substitute is seldom called upon. He told me he had been sitting by and smoking and watching the others play whist for a month now, and hoping that one of them would have a sunstroke.

We left Corinto the next morning and took the train to Lake Managua, where we were to connect with a steamer which crosses the lake to the capital. It was a beautiful ride, and for some distance ran along the sea-shore, where the ocean rolled up the beach in great waves, breaking in showers of foam upon the rocks. Then we crossed lagoons and swamps on trestles, and passed pretty thatched villages, and saw many beautiful women and girls selling candy and sugar - cane at the stations. They wore gowns that left the neck and shoulders bare, and wrapped themselves in silk shawls of solid colors, which they kept continually loosening and rearranging, tossing the ends coquettishly from one shoulder to the other, or drawing

ARBOR OF CORINTO

them closely about the figure, or like a cowl over the head. This silk shawl is the most characteristic part of the wardrobe of the native women of Central America. It is as inevitable as the mantilla of their richer sisters, and it is generally the only bit of splendor they possess. A group of them on a feast-day or Sunday, when they come marching towards you with green, purple, blue, or yellow shawls, makes a very striking picture.

These women of the pueblo in Honduras and Nicaragua were better-looking than the women of the lower classes of any country I have ever visited. They were individually more beautiful, and the proportion of beautiful women was greater. A woman there is accustomed from her childhood to carry heavy burdens on her head, and this gives to all of them an erect carriage and a fearless uplifting of the head when they walk or stand. They have never known a tight dress or a tight shoe, and they move as easily and as gracefully as an antelope. Their hair is very rich and heavy, and they oil it and comb it and braid it from morning to night, wearing it parted in the middle, and drawn tightly back over the ears, and piled upon the head in heavy braids. Their complexion is a light brown, and their eyes have the sad look which one sees in the eyes of a deer or a dog, and which is not so much the sign of any sorrow as of the lack of in-

telligence.   The women of the upper classes are
like most Spanish-American women, badly and
over dressed in a gown fashioned after some forgotten Parisian mode, with powder over their
faces, and with their hair frizzled and curled in
ridiculous profusion.   They are a very sorry contrast to a woman of the people, such as you see
standing in the doorways of the mud-huts, or
advancing towards you along the trail with an
earthen jar on her shoulder, straight of limb, and
with a firm, fine lower jaw, a low, broad forehead,
and shy, sad eyes.

Managua, the capital of Nicaragua, is a most
dismal city, built on a plain of sun-dried earth,
with houses of sun-dried earth, plazas and parks
and streets of sun-dried earth, and a mantle of
dust over all.   Even the stores that have been
painted in colors and hung with balconies have a
depressed, dirty, and discouraged air.   The streets
are as full of ruts and furrows as a country road,
the trees in the plaza are lifeless, and their leaves
shed dust instead of dew, and the people seem to
have taken on the tone of their surroundings,
and very much more of the dust than seems absolutely necessary.   We were there only two
days, and felt when we left as though we had
been camping out on a baseball diamond; and
we were sure that had we remained any longer
we should have turned into living statues of clay
when the sun shone, and of mud when it rained.

THE PRESIDENT'S HOUSE AT MANAGUA

There was no American minister or consul at Managua at the time of our visit, but the English consul took very good care of us, and acted as our interpreter when we called upon the president. Relations between the consul and President Zelaya were somewhat strained at that time, and though we knew this we told the consul to tell the president how much he was admired by the American people for having taken the stand he did against the English on the Mosquito Coast question, and that we hoped he would see that the British obtained no foothold near our canal. At which the English consul would hesitate and grin unhappily, and remark, in a hurried aside, " I'll be hanged if I'll translate that." So we continued inventing other pleasant speeches derogatory to Britons and British influence in Nicaragua until Somerset and his consul protested vigorously, and the president saw what we were doing and began to enjoy the consul's embarrassment and laughed, and the consul laughed with him, and they made up their quarrel—for the time being, at least.

Zelaya said, among other things, that if there were no other argument in favor of the Nicaragua Canal than that it would enable the United States to move her ships of war quickly from ocean to ocean, instead of being forced as she is now to make them take the long journey around Cape Horn. it would be of inestimable benefit. He also said that the only real objection that had been made in the United States to the canal came from those interested in the transcontinental railroads, who saw in its completion the destruction of their freight traffic.

He seemed to be a very able man, and more a man of the world than Bonilla, the President of Honduras, and much older in many ways. He was apparently somewhat of a philosopher, and believed, or said he did, in the survival of the fittest as applied to the occupation of his country. He welcomed the gringos, he said, and if they were better able to rule Nicaragua than her own people, he would accept that fact as inevitable and make way before them.

We returned to Corinto after wallowing in the dust-bins of Managua as joyfully as though it were a home, and we were so anxious to reach the ocean again that we left Granada and Leon, which are, so we are told, much more attractive than the capital, out of our route.

Corinto was bright and green and sunny, and the waters of the big harbor before it danced and flashed by day and radiated with phosphorescent fire by night. It was distinctly a place where it would occur to one to write up the back pages of his diary, but it was interesting at least in showing us the life of the exiles in these hot, far-away seaports among a strange people.

There was but one hotel, which happened to be

PRESIDENT ZELAYA OF NICARAGUA

a very good one with a very bad proprietor, who, I trust, will come some day to an untimely death at the end of one of his own billiard-cues. The hotel was built round a patio filled with palms and ramparts of empty bottles from the bar, covered with dust, and bearing the name of every brewer and wine-grower in Europe. The sleeping-rooms were on the second floor, and looked on the patio on one side and upon a wide covered veranda which faced the harbor on the other. The five resident gringos in Corinto lived at the hotel, and sat all day on this veranda swinging in their hammocks and swapping six-months-old magazines and tattered novels. Reading-matter assumed an importance in Corinto it had never attained before, and we read all the serial stories, of which there was never more than the fourth or sixth instalment, and the scientific articles on the Fall of the Rupee in India, or the Most Recent Developments in Electricity, and delighted in the advertisements of seeds and bicycles and baking-powders.

The top of our veranda was swept by a row of plane-trees that grew in the sandy soil of the beach below us, and under the shade of which were gathered all the idle ones of the port. There were among them thieving ships' stewards who had been marooned from passing vessels, ne'er-do-wells from the interior who were " combing the beach " and looking for work, but not so

diligently that they had seen the coffee plantations on their tramp down to the coast, and who
begged for money to take them back to "God's
country," or to the fever hospital at Panama.
With them were natives, sailors from the rolling
tug-boat they called a ship of war, and barefooted soldiers from the cartel, and longshore-
men with over-developed chests and muscles, who
toil mightily on steamer days and sleep and eat
for the ten days between as a reward.

All of these idlers gathered in the shade around
the women who sold sweet drinks and sticks of
pink-and-yellow candy. They were the public
characters of the place and the centre of all the
gossip of the town, and presided over their tables
with great dignity in freshly ironed frocks and
brilliant turbans. They were very handsome and
very clean-looking, with bare arms and shoulders,
and their hair always shone with cocoanut oil,
and was wonderfully braided and set off with
flowers stuck coquettishly over one ear. The
men used to sit around them in groups on the
bags of coffee waiting for export, and on the
boxes of barbed wire, which seemed to be the
only import. And sometimes a small boy would
buy a stick of candy or command the mixture
of a drink, and the woman would fuss over her
carved gourds, and rinse and rub them and mix
queer liquors with a whirling stick of wood that
she spun between the palms of her hands. We

would all watch the operation with great interest, the natives on the coffee-sacks and ourselves upon the balcony, and regard the small boy while he drank the concoction with envy.

The veranda had loose planks for its floor, and gaping knot-holes through which the legs of our chairs would sink suddenly, and which we could use on those occasions when we wanted to drop penknives and pencils and water on the heads of those passing below. Our companions in idleness were the German agents of the trading-houses and young Englishmen down from the mines to shake off a touch of fever, and two Americans who were taking a phonograph through Central America. Their names were Edward Morse and Charles Brackett, and we will always remember them as the only Americans we met who were taking money out of Central America and not bringing it there to lose it.

Every afternoon we all tramped a mile or two up the beach in the hot sun for the sake of a quarter of an hour of surf-bathing, which was delightful in itself, and which was rendered especially interesting by our having to share the surf with large man-eating sharks. When they came, which they were sure to do ten minutes after we had arrived, we generally gave them our share.

The phonograph men and our party did not believe in sharks: so we would venture out some distance, leaving the Englishmen and the Germans standing like sandpipers where the water was hardly up to their ankles, and keeping an anxious lookout for us and themselves. Had the sharks attempted to attack us from the land, they would have afforded excellent protection. When they all yelled at once and ran back up the beach into the bushes, we knew that they thought we had been in long enough, and we came out, and made as much noise as we could while doing so. But there would be invariably one man left behind—one man who had walked out farther than the others, and who, owing to the roar of the surf, could not hear our shrieks of terror. It was exciting to watch him from the beach diving and splashing happily by himself, and shaking the water out of his ears and hair, blissfully unconscious of the deserted waste of waters about him and of the sharp, black fin that shot like a torpedo from wave to wave. We would watch him as he turned to speak to the man who the moment before had been splashing and diving on his right, and, missing him, turn to the other side, and then whirl about and see us all dancing frantically up and down in a row along the beach, beckoning and screaming and waving our arms. We could observe even at that distance his damp hair rising on his head and his eyes starting out of their sockets as he dug his toes into the sand and pushed back the water with his arms, and worked his head and shoulders and every muscle in his whole body as though he were fighting his way through a mob of men. The water seemed very opaque at such times, and the current appeared to have turned seaward, and the distance from shore looked as though it were increasing at every step.

When night came to Corinto we would sit out on the wharf in front of the hotel and watch the fish darting through the phosphorescent waters and marking their passage with a trail of fire, or we would heave a log into it and see the sparks fly just as though we had thrown it upon a smouldering fire. One night one of the men was obliging enough to go into it for our benefit, and swam under water, sweeping great circles with his arms and legs. He was outlined as clearly in the inky depths below as though he wore a suit of spangles. Sometimes a shark or some other big fish drove a shoal of little fish towards the shore, and they would turn the whole surface of the water into half-circles of light as they took leap after leap for safety. Later in the evening we would go back to the veranda and listen to our friends the phonograph impresarios play duets on the banjo and guitar, and in return for the songs of the natives they had picked up in their wanderings we would sing to them those popular measures which had

arisen into notice since they had left civilization.

This was our life at Corinto for ten idle days,
until at last the steamer arrived, and the passengers came on shore to stretch their legs and buy
souvenirs, and the ship's steward bustled about
in search of fresh vegetables, and the lighters
plied heavily between the shore and the ship's
side, piled high with odorous sacks of coffee.
And then Morse and Brackett started with their
phonograph through Costa Rica, and we continued on to Panama, leaving the five foreign
residents of Corinto to the uninterrupted enjoy-
ment of their whist, and richer and happier
through our coming in an inaccurate knowledge
of the first verse and tune of "Tommy Atkins,"
which they shouted at us defiantly as they pulled
back from the steamer's side to their quiet haven
of exile.

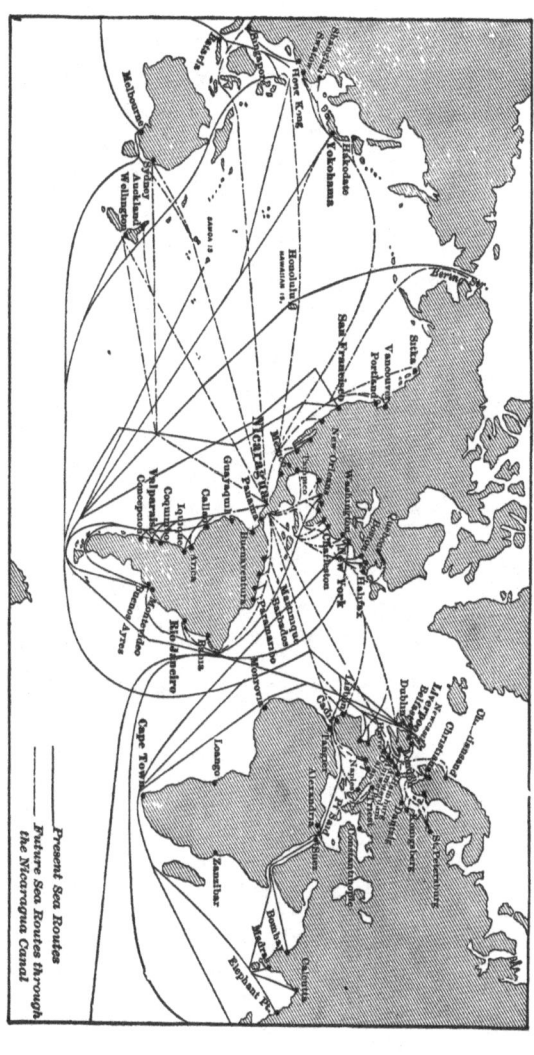

MAP OF THE WORLD SHOWING CHANGE IN TRADE ROUTES AFTER THE COMPLETION OF THE NICARAGUA
CANAL

Present Sea Routes
Future Sea Routes through
the Nicaragua Canal

ON THE ISTHMUS OF PANAMA

IF Ulysses in his wanderings had attempted to cross the Isthmus of Panama his account of the adventure would not have been filled with engineering reports or health statistics, nor would it have dwelt with horror on the irregularities of the canal company. He would have treated the isthmus in language full of imagination, and would have delivered his tale in the form of an allegory. He would have told how on such a voyage his ship came upon a strip of land joining two great continents and separating two great oceans; how he had found this isthmus guarded by a wicked dragon that exhaled poison with every breath, and that lay in wait, buried in its swamps and jungles, for sailors and travellers, who withered away and died as soon as they put foot upon the shore. But that he, warned in time by the sight of thousands of men's bones whitening on the beach, hoisted all sail and stood out to sea.

It is quite as easy to believe a story like that
as to believe the truth: that for the last century
a narrow strip of swamp land has blocked the
progress of the world; that it has joined the
peoples of two continents without permitting
them to use it as a thoroughfare; that it has
stopped the meeting of two great oceans and
the shipping of the world, and that it has killed
with its fever half of those who came to do battle
against it.   There is something almost uncanny
in the manner in which this strip of mud and
water has resisted the advance of man, as though
there really were some evil genius of the place
lurking in the morasses and brooding over the
waters, throwing out its poison like a serpent,
noiselessly and suddenly, meeting the last arrival at the very moment of his setting foot
upon the wharf, arrogant in health and hope and
ambition, and leaving him with clinched teeth
and raving with madness before the sun sets.
It is like the old Minotaur and his yearly tribute
of Greek maidens, with the difference that now
it is the lives of men that are sacrificed, and
men who are chosen from every nation of the
world, speaking every language, believing in
every religion; and to-day the end of each is
marked by a wooden plank in the Catholic
Cemetery, in the Hebrew Cemetery, in the
French Cemetery, in the English Cemetery, in
the American Cemetery, for there are acres and

DREDGES IN THE CANAL

acres of cemeteries and thousands and thousands of wooden head-stones, to which the evil spirit of the isthmus points mockingly, and says, "These are your failures."

The fields of Waterloo and Gettysburg saw a sacrifice of life but little greater than these fifty miles of swamp land between North and South America have seen, and certainly they saw no such inglorious defeats, without a banner flying or a comrade cheering, or the roar of musketry and cannon to inspire the soldiers who fell in the unequal battle. Those who died striving to save the Holy Land from the unspeakable Turk were comforted by the promise of a glorious immortality, and it must have been gratifying in itself to have been described as a Crusader, and to have worn the red cross upon one's shoulder. And, in any event, a man who would not fight for his religion or his country without promises or pensions is hardly worthy of consideration. But these young soldiers of the transit and sailors of the dredging-scow had no promises or sentiment to inspire them; they were not fighting for the boundaries of their country, but redeeming a bit of No Man's Land; not doing battle for their God, but merely digging a canal. And it must strike every one that those of them who fell doing their duty in the sickly yellow mist of Panama and along the gloomy stretches of the Chagres River deserve a better monument to their memories than the wooden slabs in the cemeteries.

It is strange that not only nature, but man also, should have selected the same little spot on the earth's surface in which to show to the world exactly how disagreeable and unpleasant they can make themselves when they choose. It seems almost as though the isthmus were unholy ground, and that there was a curse upon it. Some one should invent a legend to explain this, and tell how one of the priests who came over with Columbus put the ban of the Church upon the land for some affront by its people to the voyagers, and so placed it under a curse forever. For those whom the fever did not kill the canal company robbed, and the ruin that came to the peasants of France was as irredeemable as the ravages of the fever, and the scandal that spattered almost every public man in Paris exposed rottenness and corruption as far advanced as that in the green-coated pools along the Rio Grande.

Ruins are always interesting, but the ruins of Panama fill one only with melancholy and disgust, and the relics of this gigantic swindle can only inspire you with a contempt for yourself and your fellow-men, and you blush at the evidences of barefaced rascality about you. And even the honest efforts of those who are now in charge, and who are trying to save what

THE BAY OF PANAMA

remains, and once more to build up confidence in the canal, reminded me of the town councillors of Johnstown who met in a freight depot to decide what was to be done with the town and those of its inhabitants that had not been swept out of existence.

There are forty-eight miles of railroad across the isthmus, stretching from the town of Panama on the Pacific side to that of Colon—or Aspinwall, as it was formerly called—on the Caribbean Sea. The canal starts a little north of the town of Panama, in the mouth of the Rio Grande, and runs along on one side or the other of the railroad to the port of Colon. The Chagres River starts about the middle of the isthmus, and follows the route of the canal in an easterly direction, until it empties itself into the Caribbean Sea a little north of Colon.

The town of Panama, as you approach it from the bay, reminds you of an Italian seaport, owing to the balconies which overhang the water and the colored house-fronts and projecting red roofs. As seen from the inside, the town is like any other Spanish-American city of the second class. There are fiacres that rattle and roll through the clean but narrow streets behind undersized ponies that always move at a gallop; there are cool, dark shops open to the streets, and hundreds of negroes and Chinese coolies, and a handsome plaza, and some very large municipal buildings of five stories, which appeared to us, after our experience with a dead level of one-story huts, to tower as high as the Auditorium. Panama, as a town, and considered by itself, and not in connection with the canal, reminded me of a Western county-seat after the boom had left it. There appeared to be nothing going forward and nothing to do. The men sat at the cafés during the day and talked of the past, and went to a club at night. We saw nothing of the women, but they seem to have a greater degree of free-dom than their sisters in other parts of Spanish America, owing, no doubt, to the cosmopolitan nature of the inhabitants of Panama.

But the city, and the people in it, interest you chiefly because of the canal; and even the ruins of the Spanish occupation, and the tales of buc-caneers and of bloody battles and buried treas-ure, cannot touch you so nearly as do the great, pretentious building of the company and the stories of De Lesseps' visit, and the ceremonies and feastings and celebrations which inaugurated the greatest failure of modern times.

The new director of the canal company put a tug at our disposal, and sent us orders that per-mitted us to see as much of the canal as has been completed from the Pacific side. But before pre-senting our orders we drove out from the city one afternoon and began a personally conducted inspection of the machine-shops.

PANAMA CANAL ON THE PACIFIC SIDE

We had read of the pathetic spectacle presented by thousands of dollars' worth of locomotive
engines and machinery lying rotting and rusting
in the swamps, and as it had interested us when
we had read of it, we were naturally even more anxious to see it with our own eyes.   We, however,
did not see any machinery rusting, nor any locomotives lying half buried in the mud.   All the
locomotives that we saw were raised from the
ground on ties and protected with a wooden shed,
and had been painted and oiled and cared for as
they would have been in the Baldwin Locomotive Works.   We found the same state of things
in the great machine-works, and though none of
us knew a turning-lathe from a sewing-machine,
we could at least understand that certain wheels
should make other wheels move if everything
was in working order, and so we made the wheels
go round, and punched holes in sheets of iron
with steel rods, and pierced plates, and scraped
iron bars, and climbed to shelves twenty and
thirty feet from the floor, only to find that each
bit and screw in each numbered pigeon-hole was
as sharp and covered as thick with oil as though
it had been in use that morning.

This was not as interesting as it would have
been had we seen what the other writers who
have visited the isthmus saw.   And it would have
given me a better chance for descriptive writing
had I found the ruins of gigantic dredging-ma-

chines buried in the morasses, and millions of dollars' worth of delicate machinery blistering and rusting under the palm-trees; but, as a rule, it is better to describe things just as you saw them, and not as it is the fashion to see them, even though your way be not so picturesque.

As a matter of fact, the care the company was taking of its machinery and its fleet of dredging-scows and locomotives struck me as being much more pathetic than the sight of the same instruments would have been had we found them abandoned to the elements and the mud. For it was like a general pipe-claying his cross-belt and polishing his buttons after his army had been routed and killed, and he had lost everything, including honor.

There was a little village of whitewashed huts on the southern bank of the Rio Grande, where

HUTS OF WORKMEN EMPLOYED ON THE CANAL

the men lived who take care of the fleet and the machine-shop, and it was as carefully kept and as clean as a graveyard. Before the crash came the quarters of the men used to ring with their yells at night, and the music of guitars and banjos came from the open doors of cafés and drinking-booths, and a pistol-shot meant no more than a momentary punctuation of the night's pleasure. Those were great days, and there were thousands of men where there are now a score, and a line of light and deviltry ran from the canal's mouth for miles back to the city, where it blazed into a great fire of dissolute pleasure and excitement. In those days men were making fortunes in a night, and by ways as dark as night—by furnishing machinery that could not even be put together, by supplying blocks of granite that cost more in freight than bars of silver, by kidnapping workmen for the swamps, and by the simple methods of false accounts and credits. And while some were growing rich, others were living with the fear of sudden death before their eyes, and drinking the native rum that they might forget it, and throwing their wages away on the roulette-tables, and eating and drinking and making merry in the fear that they might die on the morrow.

Mr. Wells, an American engineer, was in charge of the company's flotilla, and waited for us at the wharf.

"I saw you investigating our engines," he

said. "That's all right. Only tell the truth about what you see, and we won't mind."

We stood on the bow of the tug and sped up the length of the canal between great dredging-machines that towered as high above us as the bridge of an ocean liner, and that weighed apparently as much as a battle-ship. The decks of some of them were split with the heat, and there were shutters missing from the cabin windows, but the monster machinery was intact, and the wood-work was freshly painted and scrubbed. They reminded me of a line of old ships of war at rest in some navy-yard. They represent in money value, even as they are to-day, five million francs. Beyond them on either side stretched low green bushes, through which the Rio Grande bent and twisted, and beyond the bushes were high hills and the Pacific Ocean, into which the sun set, leaving us cold and depressed.

Except for the bubbling of the water under our bow there was not a sound to disturb the silence that hung above the narrow canal and the green bushes that rose from a bed of water. I thought of the entrance of the Suez Canal, as I had seen it at Port Said and at Ismaïlia, with great P. & O. steamers passing down its length, and troop-ships showing hundreds of white helmets above the sides, and tramp steamers and sailing-vessels flying every flag, and com-

THE TOP OF A DREDGE

pared it and its scenes of life and movement with this dreary waste before us, with the idle dredges rearing their iron girders to the sky, the engineers' sign-posts half smothered in the water and the mud, and with a naked fisherman paddling noiselessly down the canal with his eyes fixed on the water, his hollowed log canoe the only floating vessel in what should have been the highway of the world.

There were about eight hundred men in all working along the whole length of the canal while we were there, instead of the twelve thousand that once made the place hum with activity. But the work the twelve thousand accomplished remains, and the stranger is surprised to find that there is so much of it and that it is so well done. It looks to his ignorant eyes as though only a little more energy and a greater amount of honesty would be necessary to open the canal to traffic; but experts will tell him that one hundred million dollars will have to be expended and seven or eight years of honest work done before that ditch can be dug and France hold a Kiel celebration of her own.

But before that happens every citizen of the United States should help to open the Nicaragua Canal to the world under the protection and the virtual ownership of his own country.

Our stay in Panama was shortened somewhat on account of our having taken too great an in-

terest in the freedom of a young lawyer and
diplomat, who was arrested while we were there,
charged with being one of the leaders of the
revolution.

He was an acquaintance of Lloyd Griscom's,
who took an interest in the young rebel because
they had both been in the diplomatic service
abroad. One afternoon, while Griscom and the
lawyer were sitting together in the office of the
latter, five soldiers entered the place and ordered
the suspected revolutionist to accompany them
to the cartel. As he happened to know something of the law, he protested that they must
first show him a warrant, and while two of them
went out for the warrant and the others kept
watch in the outer office Griscom mapped out a
plan of escape. The lawyer's office hung over
the Bay of Panama, and Griscom's idea was that
he should, under the protection of the darkness,
slip down a rope from the window to a small
boat below and be rowed out to the *Barracouta*,
of the Pacific Mail Company's line, which was
listed to sail that same evening up the coast.
The friends of the rebel were sent for, and with
their assistance Griscom made every preparation
for the young rebel's escape, and then came to
the hotel and informed Somerset and myself of
what he had done, and asked us to aid in what
was to follow. We knew nothing of the rights
or the wrongs of the revolutionists, but we con-

STREET SCENE IN PANAMA

sidered that a man who was going down a rope into a small boat while three soldiers sat waiting for him in an outer room was performing a sporting act that called for our active sympathy. So we followed Griscom to his friend's office, and, having passed the soldiers, were ushered into his presence and introduced to him and his friends. He was a little man, but was not at all alarmed, nor did he pose or exhibit any braggadocio, as a man of weaker calibre might have done under the circumstances. When we offered to hold the rope for him, or to block up the doors so that the soldiers might not see what was going forward, he thanked us with such grateful politeness that he made me feel rather ashamed of myself ; for my interest in the matter up to that point had not been a very serious or a high one. Indeed, I did not even know the gentleman's name. But as we did not know the names of the government people against whom he was plotting either, we felt that we could not be accused of partiality.

The prisoner did not want his wife to know what had happened, and so sent her word that important legal business would detain him at the office, and that his dinner was to be brought to him there. The rope by which he was to escape was smuggled past the soldiers under the napkin which covered this dinner. It was then seven o'clock and nearly dark, and as our rebel friend feared our presence might excite suspicion, he asked us to go away, and requested us to return in half an hour. It would then be quite dark, and the attempt to escape could be made with greater safety.

But the alcalde during our absence spoiled what might have been an excellent story by rushing in and carrying the diplomat off to jail. When we returned we found the office locked and guarded, and as we walked away, in doubt as to whether he had escaped or had been arrested, we found that the soldiers were following us. As this continued throughout the evening we went across the isthmus the next morning to Colon, the same soldiers accompanying us on our way.

The ship of war *Atlanta* was at Colon, and as we had met her officers at Puerto Cortez, in Honduras, we went on board and asked them to see that we were not shot against church walls or hung. They were exceedingly amused, and promised us ample protection, and though we did not need it on that occasion, I was impressed with the comforting sense that comes to a traveller from the States when he knows that one of our White Squadron is rolling at anchor in the harbor. And later, when Griscom caught the Chagres fever, we had every reason to be grateful for the presence in the harbor of the *Atlanta*, as her officers, led by Dr. Bartolette and

THE CANAL IN THE INTERIOR

his assistant surgeon, Mr. Moore, helped him through his sickness, visiting him daily with the greatest kindness and good-will.

Colon did not impress us very favorably. It is a large town of wooden houses, with a floating population of Jamaica negroes and a few Chinese. The houses built for the engineers of the canal stretch out along a point at either side of a double row of magnificent palms, which terminate at the residence intended for De Lesseps. It is now falling into decay. In front of it, facing the sea, is a statue of Columbus protecting the Republic of Colombia, represented by an Indian girl, who is crouching under his outstretched arm. This monument was presented to the United States of Colombia by the Empress Eugenie, and the statue is, in its fallen state, with its pedestal shattered by the many storms and time, significant of the fallen fortunes of that great lady herself. If Columbus could have protected Colombia from the French as he is in the French statue protecting her from all the world, she would now be the richest and most important of Central-American republics.

Colon seems to be owned entirely by the Panama Railroad Company, a monopoly that conducts its affairs with even more disregard for the public than do other monopolies in better-known localities. The company makes use of the seaport as a freight-yard, and its locomotives run the length of the town throughout the entire day, blowing continually on their whistles and ringing their bells, so that there is little peace for the just or the unjust. We were exceedingly relieved when the doctors agreed that Griscom was ready to put to sea again, and we were able to turn from the scene of the great scandal and its fever fields to the mountains of Venezuela, and of Caracas in particular.

THE PARIS OF SOUTH AMERICA

SHOVED off by itself in a corner of Central Park on the top of a wooded hill, where only the people who live in the high apartment - houses at Eighty-first Street can see it, is an equestrian statue. It is odd, bizarre, and inartistic, and suggests in size and pose that equestrian statue to General Jackson which mounts guard before the White House in Washington. It shows a chocolate-cream soldier mastering with one hand a rearing rocking-horse, and with the other pointing his sword towards an imaginary enemy.

Sometimes a "sparrow" policeman saunters up the hill and looks at the statue with unenlightened eyes, and sometimes a nurse - maid seeks its secluded site, and sits on the pedestal below it while the children of this free republic play unconcernedly in its shadow. On the base of this big statue is carved the name of Simon Bolivar, the Liberator of Venezuela.

Down on the northeastern coast of South America, in Caracas, the capital of the United States of Venezuela, there is a pretty little plaza, called the Plaza Washington. It is not at all an important plaza; it is not floored for hundreds of yards with rare mosaics like the Plaza de Bolivar, nor lit by swinging electric lights, and the president's band never plays there. But it has a fresh prettiness and restfulness all its own, and the narrow gravel paths are clean and trim, and the grass grows rich and high, and the branches of the trees touch and interlace and form a green roof over all, except in the very centre, where there stands open to the blue sky a statue of Washington, calm, dignified, beneficent, and paternal. It is Washington the statesman, not the soldier. The sun of the tropics beats down upon his shoulders; the palms rustle and whisper pleasantly above his head. From the barred windows of the yellow and blue and pink houses that line the little plaza dark-eyed, dark-skinned women look out sleepily, but understandingly, at the grave face of the North American Bolivar; and even the policeman, with his red blanket and Winchester carbine, comprehends when the gringos stop and take off their hats and make a low bow to the father of their country in his pleasant place of exile.

Other governments than those of the United States of America and the United States of

STATUE OF SIMON BOLIVAR, CARACAS

Venezuela have put up statues to their great men in foreign capitals, but the careers of Washington and Bolivar bear so striking a resemblance, and the histories of the two countries of which they are the respective fathers are so much alike, that they might be written in parallel columns. And so it seems especially appropriate that these monuments to these patriots should stand in each of the two continents on either side of the dividing states of Central America.

It will offend no true Venezuelan to-day if it be said of his country that the most interesting man in it is a dead one, for he will allow no one to go further than himself in his admiration for Bolivar; and he has done so much to keep his memory fresh by circulating portraits of him on every coin and stamp of the country, by placing his statue at every corner, and by hanging his picture in every house, that he cannot blame the visitor if his strongest impression of Venezuela is of the young man who began at thirty-three to liberate five republics, and who conquered a territory more than one-third as great as the whole of Europe.

In 1811 Venezuela declared her independence of the mother-country of Spain, and her great men put this declaration in writing and signed it, and the room in which it was signed is still kept sacred, as is the room where our declaration was signed in Independence Hall. But the two men who were to make these declarations worth something more than the parchment upon which they were written were not among the signers. Their work was still to come, and it was much the same kind of work, and carried on in much the same spirit of indomitable energy under the most cruel difficulties, and with a few undrilled troops against an army of veterans. It was marked by brilliant and sudden marches and glorious victories ; and where Washington suffered in the snows of Valley Forge, or pushed his way through the floating ice of the Delaware, young Bolivar marched under fierce tropical suns, and cut his path through jungle and swamp-lands, and over the almost impenetrable fastnesses of the Andes.

Their difficulties were the same and their aim was the same, but the characters of the two men were absolutely and entirely different, for Bolivar was reckless, impatient of advice, and even foolhardy. What Washington was we know.

The South-American came of a distinguished Spanish family, and had been educated as a courtier and as a soldier in the mother-country, though his heart remained always with his own people, and he was among the first to take up arms to set them free. Unless you have seen the country through which he led his men, and have measured the mountains he climbed with

STATUE OF WASHINGTON DECORATED WITH FLORAL WREATHS
BY THE VENEZUELANS

his few followers, it is quite impossible to understand the immensity of the task he accomplished. Even to-day a fast steamer cannot reach Callao from Panama under seven days, and yet Bolivar made the same distance and on foot, starting from the South Atlantic, and continuing on across the continent to the Pacific side, and then on down the coast into Peru, living on his way upon roots and berries, sleeping on the ground wrapped in a blanket, riding on muleback or climbing the steep trail on foot, and freeing on his way Venezuela, Colombia, Ecuador, Bolivia, and finally Peru, the home of the Incas.

The history of this campaign is one too glorious and rich in incident and color to be crowded into a few pages, and the character of its chief actor too varied, and his rise and fall too dramatic, to be dismissed, as it must be here, in a few paragraphs. But every American who loves a hero and who loves a lover—and Bolivar was very much of both, and perhaps too much of the latter—should read the life of this young man who freed a country rich in brave men, who made some of these who were much his senior in years his lieutenants, and who, after risking his life upon many battle-fields and escaping several attempts at assassination, died at last deserted except by a few friends, and with a heart broken by the ingratitude of the people he had led out of captivity.

It is difficult to find out, even in his own country, why the Venezuelans, after heaping Bolivar with honors and elevating him to the place of a god, should have turned against him, and driven him into exile at Santa Marta. Some will tell you that he tried to make himself dictator over the countries which he had freed ; others say that it was because he had refused to be a dictator that the popular feeling went against him, and that when the people in the madness of their new-found freedom cried, "Thou hast rid us of kings; be thou king," he showed them their folly, and sought his old home, and died there before the reaction came, which was to sweep him back once more and forever into the place of the popular hero of South America.

It was sixteen years after his death that a hero-worshipping friend was brave enough to commission an artist to design a statue to his memory. On the neck of this statue the artist hung the representation of a miniature in the shape of a medallion, which had been given to Bolivar by the family of Washington. On the reverse was a lock of Washington's hair and the inscription, "This portrait of the founder of liberty in North America is presented by his adopted son to him who has acquired equal glory in South America."

Some one asked why the artist had stripped from the breast of Bolivar all of the other

W. W. Russell,   Sen Allen Thomas,   W. S. Bird,
Sec'y of Legation   U. S. Minister   Consular Agent

DECORATION OF THE STATUE OF BOLIVAR AT CARACAS, VENE
ZUELA, DECEMBER 18, 1895, BY AMERICAN RESIDENTS

medals and stars that had been given him by
different countries in the hour of his triumph,
and the artist answered that he had done as his
patron and the friend of Bolivar thought would
best please his hero.   And ever after that it was
decreed that every bust or statue or engraving
of the Liberator should show him with this
portrait of Washington hanging by a ribbon
about his neck; and so you will see in the
National Portrait Gallery that while the coats
of his lieutenants glitter with orders and crosses, Bolivar's bears this medal only.   It was his
greatest pride, and he considered it his chief
glory.   And the manner of its bestowal was
curiously appropriate.   In 1824 General Lafayette returned to this country as the guest of
the nation, and a banquet was given to him by
Congress, at which the memory of Washington
and the deeds of his French lieutenant were
honored again and again.   It was while the
enthusiasm and rejoicings of this celebration
were at their height that Henry Clay rose in
his place and asked the six hundred Americans
before him to remember that while they were
enjoying the benefits of free institutions founded
by the bravery and patriotism of their fore-
fathers, their cousins and neighbors in the southern continent were struggling to obtain that same
independence.

   " No nation, no generous Lafayette," he cried,

" has come to their aid; alone and without help they have sustained their glorious cause, trusting to its justice, and with the assistance only of

SIMON BOLIVAR

their bravery, their deserts, and their Andes— and one man, Simon Bolivar, the Washington of South America."

And you can imagine the six hundred Americans jumping to their feet and cheering the

VIEW OF LA GUAYRA

name of the young soldier, and the French marquis eagerly asking that he might be the one to send him some token of their sympathy and admiration. Lafayette forwarded the portrait of Washington to Bolivar, who valued it so highly that the people who loved him valued the man he worshipped; and to-day you will see in Caracas streets and squares and houses named after Washington, and portraits of Washington crossing the Delaware, and Washington on horseback, and Washington at Mount Vernon, hanging in almost every shop and café in the capital. And the next time you ride in Central Park you might turn your bicycle, or tell the man on the box to turn the horses, into that little curtain of trees, and around the hill where the odd-looking statue stands, and see if you cannot feel some sort of sympathy and pay some tribute to this young man who loved like a hero, and who fought like a hero, with the fierceness of the tropical sun above him, and whose inspiration was the calm, grave parent of your own country.

Bolivar's country is the republic of South America that stands nearest to New York, and when people come to know more concerning it, I am sure they will take to visiting it and its capital, the "Paris of South America," in the winter months, as they now go to southern Europe or to the Mediterranean.

There are many reasons for their doing so.

In the first place, it can be reached in less than six days, and it is the only part of South America to which one can go without first crossing the Isthmus of Panama and then taking a long trip down the western coast, or sailing for nearly a month along the eastern coast; and it is a wonderfully beautiful country, and its cities of Caracas and Valencia are typical of the best South-American cities. When you have seen them you have an intelligent idea of what the others are like; and when you read about revolutions in Rio Janeiro, or Valparaiso, or Buenos Ayres, you will have in your mind's eye the background for all of these dramatic uprisings, and you will feel superior to other people who do not know that the republic of Venezuela is larger than France, Spain, and Portugal together, and that the inhabitants of this great territory are less in number than those of New York city.

La Guayra is the chief seaport of Venezuela. It lies at the edge of a chain of great mountains, where they come down to wet their feet in the ocean, and Caracas, the capital, is stowed away three thousand feet higher up behind these mountains, and could only be bombarded in time of war by shells that would rise like rockets and drop on the other side of the mountains, and so cover a distance quite nine miles away from the vessel that fired them. Above La Guayra, on the hill, is a little fortress which was

THE RAILROAD UP THE MOUNTAIN

once the residence of the Spanish governor when Venezuela was a colony of Spain. It is of interest now chiefly because Charles Kingsley describes it in *Westward Ho!* as the fortress in which the Rose of Devon was imprisoned. Past this fortress, and up over the mountains to the capital, are a mule-trail and an ancient wagon-road and a modern railway.

It is a very remarkable railroad; its tracks cling to the perpendicular surface of the mountain like the tiny tendrils of a vine on a stone-wall, and the trains creep and crawl along the edge of its precipices, or twist themselves into the shape of a horseshoe magnet, so that the engineer on the locomotive can look directly across a bottomless chasm into the windows of the last car. The view from this train, while it pants and puffs on its way to the capital, is the most beautiful combination of sea and plain and mountain that I have ever seen. There are higher mountains and more beautiful, perhaps, but they run into a brown prairie or into a green plain; and there are as beautiful views of the ocean, only you have to see them from the level of the ocean itself, or from a chalk-cliff with the downs behind you and the white sand at your feet. But nowhere else in the world have I seen such magnificent and noble mountains running into so beautiful and green a plain, and beyond that the great blue stretches of the sea. When you look down from

the car-platform you see first, stretching three
thousand feet below you, the great green ribs of
the mountain and its valleys and waterways leading into a plain covered with thousands and thousands of royal palms, set so far apart that you
can distinguish every broad leaf and the full
length of the white trunk.   Among these are the
red-roofed and yellow villages, and beyond them
again the white line of breakers disappearing and
reappearing against the blue as though some one
were wiping out a chalk-line and drawing it in
again, and then the great ocean weltering in the
heat and stretching as far as the eye can see, and
touching a sky so like it in color that the two are
joined in a curtain of blue on which the ships
seem to lie flat, like painted pictures on a wall.
You pass through clouds on your way up that
leave the trees and rocks along the track damp
and shining as after a heavy dew, and at some
places you can peer through them from the steps
of the car down a straight fall of three thousand
feet.   When you have climbed to the top of the
mountain, you see below you on the other side
the beautiful valley in which lies the city of Caracas, cut up evenly by well-kept streets, and diversi-
fied by the towers of churches and public buildings and open plazas, with the white houses and
gardens of the coffee-planters lying beyond the
city at the base of the mountains.

Venezuela, after our experiences of Central

COURT-YARD OF A HOUSE IN CARACAS

America, was like a return to civilization after months on the alkali plains of Texas. We found Caracas to be a Spanish-American city of the first class, with a suggestion of the boulevards, and Venezuela a country that possessed a history of her own, and an Academy of wise men and artists, and a Pantheon for her heroes. I suppose we should have known that this was so before we visited Venezuela; but as we did not, we felt as though we were discovering a new country for ourselves. It was interesting to find statues of men of whom none of us had ever heard, and who were distinguished for something else than military successes, men who had made discoveries in science and medicine, and who had written learned books; to find the latest devices for comfort of a civilized community, and with them the records of a fierce struggle for independence, a long period of disorganization, where the Church had the master-hand, and then a rapid advance in the habits and customs of enlightened nations. There are the most curious combinations and contrasts, showing on one side a pride of country and an eagerness to emulate the customs of stable governments, and on the other evidences of the Southern hot-blooded temperament and dislike of restraint.

On the corner of the principal plaza stands the cathedral, with a tower. Ten soldiers took refuge in this tower four years ago, during the last revolution, and they made so determined a fight from that point of vantage that in order to dislodge them it was found necessary to build a fire in the tower and smoke them out with the fumes of sulphur. These ten soldiers were the last to make a stand within the city, and when they fell, from the top of the tower, smothered to death, the revolution was at an end. This incident of warfare is of value when you contrast the thing done with its environment, and know that next to the cathedral - tower are confectionery - shops such as you find on Regent Street or upper Broadway, that electric lights surround the cathedral, and that tram-cars run past it on rails sunk below the surface of the roadway and over a better street than any to be found in New York city.

Even without acquaintances among the people of the capital there are enough public show-places in Caracas to entertain a stranger for a fortnight. It is pleasure enough to walk the long, narrow streets under brilliantly colored awnings, between high one and two story houses, painted in blues and pinks and greens, and with overhanging red-tiled roofs and projecting iron balconies and open iron - barred windows, through which you gain glimpses beyond of cool interiors and beautiful courts and gardens filled with odd-looking plants around a splashing fountain.

The ladies of Caracas seem to spend much of

THE MARKET OF CARACAS

their time sitting at these windows, and are always there in the late afternoons, when they dress themselves and arrange their hair for the evening, and put a little powder on their faces, and take their places in the cushioned window-seats as though they were in their box at the opera. And though they are within a few inches of the passers-by on the pavement, they can look through them and past them, and are as oblivious of their presence as though they were invisible. In the streets are strings of mules carrying bags of coffee or buried beneath bales of fodder, and jostled by open fiacres, with magnificent coachmen on the box - seat in top - boots and gold trimmings to their hats and coats, and many soldiers, on foot and mounted, hurrying along at a quick step in companies, or strolling leisurely alone. They wear blue uniforms with scarlet trousers and facings, and the president's bodyguard are in white duck and high black boots, and are mounted on magnificent horses.

There are three great buildings in Caracas—the Federal Palace, the Opera-house, and the Pantheon, which was formerly a church, and which has been changed into a receiving-vault and a memorial for the great men of the country. Here, after three journeys, the bones of Bolivar now rest. The most interesting of these buildings is the Federal Palace. It is formed around a great square filled with flowers and fountains, and lit

with swinging electric lights. It is the handsom-
est building in Caracas, and within its four sides
are the chambers of the upper and lower branches of the legislature, the offices of the different
departments of state, and the reception-hall of
the president, in which is the National Portrait
Gallery. The palace is light and unsubstantial-
looking, like a canvas palace in a theatre, and
suggests the casino at a French watering-place.
It is painted in imitation of stone, and the statues are either of plaster-of-paris or of wood,
painted white to represent marble. But the theatrical effect is in keeping with the colored walls
and open fronts of the other buildings of the city,
and is not out of place in this city of such dramatic incidents.

The portraits in the state-room of the palace
immortalize the features of fierce-looking, dark-
faced generals, with old-fashioned high-standing
collars of gold-braid, and green uniforms. Strange
and unfamiliar names are printed beneath these
portraits, and appear again painted in gold letters on a roll of honor which hangs from the ceil-
ing, and which faces a list of the famous battles
for independence. High on this roll of honor
are the names "General O'Leary" and "Colonel Fergurson," and among the portraits are the
faces of two blue-eyed, red-haired young men,
with fair skin and broad chests and shoulders,
one wearing the close-clipped whiskers of the

PRESIDENT CRESPO, OF VENEZUELA

last of the Georges, and the other the long Dun-
dreary whiskers of the Crimean wars. Whether
the Irish general and the English colonel gave
their swords for the sake of the cause of independence or fought for the love of fighting, I do

LEGISLATIVE BUILDING, CARACAS

not know, but they won the love of the Spanish-
Americans by the service they rendered, no matter what their motives may have been for serving.
Many people tell you proudly that they are descended from "O'Leari," and the names of the
two foreigners are as conspicuous on pedestals
and tablets of honor as are their smiling blue

eyes and red cheeks among the thin-visaged, dark-skinned faces of their brothers-in-arms.

At one end of the room is an immense painting of a battle, and the other is blocked by as large a picture showing Bolivar dictating to members of Congress, who have apparently ridden out into the field to meet him, and are holding an impromptu session beneath the palm leaves of an Indian hut. The dome of the chamber, which latter is two hundred feet in length, is covered with an immense panorama, excellently well done, showing the last of the battles of the Venezuelans against the Spaniards, in which the figures are life-size and the action most spirited, and the effect of color distinctly decorative. These paintings in the National Gallery would lead you to suppose that there was nothing but battles in the history of Venezuela, and that her great men were all soldiers, but the talent of the artists who have painted these scenes and the actors in them corrects the idea. Among these artists are Arturo Michelena, who has exhibited at the World's Fair, and frequently at the French Salon, from which institution he has received a prize, M. Tovar y Tovar, A. Herrea Toro, and Cristobal Rojas.

It was that "Illustrious American, Guzman Blanco," one of the numerous presidents of Venezuela, and probably the best known, who was responsible for most of the public buildings of

THE PRESIDENT'S BODY-GUARD OF COWBOYS

the capital. These were originally either con-
vents or monasteries, which he converted, after
his war with the Church, into the Federal Palace, the Opera-house, and a university. Each of
these structures covers so much valuable ground,
and is situated so advantageously in the very
heart of the city, that one gets a very good idea
of how powerful the Church element must have
been before Guzman overthrew it.

He was a peculiar man, apparently, and possessed of much force and of a progressive spirit,
combined with an overmastering vanity. The
city was at its gayest under his régime, and he
encouraged the arts and sciences by creating various bodies of learned men, by furnishing the
nucleus for a national museum, by subsidizing
the Opera-house, and by granting concessions
to foreign companies which were of quite too
generous a nature to hold good, and which now
greatly encumber and embarrass his successors.
But while he was president, and before he
went to live in luxurious exile on the Avenue
Kléber, which seems to be the resting-place of
all South American presidents, he did much to
make the country prosperous and its capital attractive, and he was determined that the people
should know that he was the individual who accomplished these things. With this object he
had fifteen statues erected to himself in different
parts of the city, and more tablets than one can

count. Each statue bore an inscription telling
that it was erected to that " Illustrious American, Guzman Blanco," and every new bridge and
road and public building bore a label to say that
it was Guzman Blanco who was responsible for
its existence. The idea of a man erecting statues to himself struck the South-American mind
as extremely humorous, and one night all the
statues were sawed off at the ankles, and to-day
there is not one to be seen, and only raw places
in the walls to show where the memorial tablets
hung. But you cannot wipe out history by pulling down columns or effacing inscriptions, and
Guzman Blanco undoubtedly did do much for
his country, even though at the same time he
was doing a great deal for Guzman Blanco.

Guzman was followed in rapid succession by
three or four other presidents and dictators, who
filled their pockets with millions and then fled
the country, only waiting until their money was
first safely out of it. Then General Crespo, who
had started his revolution with seven men, finally overthrew the government's forces, and was
elected president, and has remained in office
ever since. To set forth with seven followers to
make yourself president of a country as large as
France, Portugal, and Spain together requires a
great deal of confidence and courage. General
Crespo is a fighter, and possesses both. It was
either he or one of his generals—the story is told

BAPTIZING INDIANS AT A VENEZUELAN STATION ON THE CUYUNI RIVER

of both — who, when he wanted arms for his cowboys, bade them take off their shirts and grease their bodies and rush through the camp of the enemy in search of them. He told them to hold their left hands out as they ran, and whenever their fingers slipped on a greased body they were to pass it by, but when they touched a man wearing a shirt they were to cut him down with their machetes. In this fashion three hundred of his plainsmen routed two thousand of the regular troops, and captured all of their rifles and ammunition. The idea that when you want arms the enemy is the best person from whom to take them is excellent logic, and that charge of the half-naked men, armed only with their knives, through the sleeping camp is Homeric in its magnificence.

Crespo is more at home when fighting in the field than in the council-chamber of the Yellow House, which is the White House of the republic; but that may be because he prefers fighting to governing, and a man generally does best what he likes best to do. He is as simple in his habits to-day as when he was on the march with his seven revolutionists, and goes to bed at eight in the evening, and is deep in public business by four the next morning; many an unhappy minister has been called to an audience at sunrise. The president neither smokes nor drinks; he is grave and dignified, with that dignity which enormous size gives, and his greatest pleasure is to take a holiday and visit his ranch, where he watches the round-up of his cattle and gallops over his thousands of acres. He is the idol of the cowboys, and has a body-guard composed of some of the men of this class. I suppose they are very much like our own cowboys, but the citizens of the capital look upon them as the Parisians regarded Napoleon's Mamelukes, and tell you in perfect sincerity that when they charge at night their eyes flash fire in a truly terrifying manner.

I saw the president but once, and then but for a few moments. He was at the Yellow House and holding a public reception, to which every one was admitted with a freedom that betokened absolute democracy. When my turn came he talked awhile through Colonel Bird, our consul, but there was no chance for me to gain any idea of him except that he was very polite, as are all Venezuelans, and very large. They tell a story of him which illustrates his character. He was riding past the university when a group of students hooted and jeered at him, not because of his politics, but because of his origin. A policeman standing by, aroused to indignation by this insult to the president, fired his revolver into the crowd. Crespo at once ordered the man's arrest for shooting at a citizen with no sufficient provocation, and rode on his way without even giving a glance at his tor-

A TYPICAL HUNTING-PARTY IN VENEZUELA

mentors. The incident seemed to show that he was too big a man to allow the law to be broken even in his own defence, or, at least, big enough not to mind the taunts of ill-bred children.

The boys of the university are taken very seriously by the people of Caracas, as are all boys in that country, where a child is listened to, if he be a male child, with as much grave politeness as though it were a veteran who was speaking.   The effect is not good, and the boys, especially of the university, grow to believe that they are very important factors in the affairs of the state, when, as a matter of fact, they are only the cat's-paws of clever politicians, who use them whenever they want a demonstration and do not wish to appear in it themselves. So these boys are sent forth shouting into the streets, and half the people cheer them on, and the children themselves think they are patriots or liberators, or something equally important.

I obtained a rather low opinion of them because they stoned an unfortunate American photographer who was taking pictures in the quadrangles, and because I was so far interested in them as to get a friend of mine to translate for me the sentences and verses they had written over the walls of their college. The verses were of a political character, but so indecent that the interpreter was much embarrassed ; the single sentences were attacks, anonymous, of course, on fellow-students. As the students of the University of Venezuela step directly from college life into public life, their training is of some interest and importance. And I am sure that the Venezuelan fathers would do much better by their sons if they would cease to speak of the university in awe-stricken tones as "the hotbed of liberty," but would rather take away the boys' revolvers and teach them football, and thrash them soundly whenever they caught them soiling the walls of their alma mater with nasty verses.

There are some beautiful drives around Caracas, out in the country among the coffee plantations, and one to a public garden that overlooks the city, upon which President Crespo has spent much thought and money. But the most beautiful feature of Caracas, and one that no person who has visited that place will ever forget, is the range of mountains above it, which no president can improve. They are smooth and bare of trees and of a light-green color, except in the waterways, where there are lines of darker green, and the clouds change their aspect continually, covering them with shadows or floating over them from valley to valley, and hovering above a high peak like the white smoke of a volcano.

I do not know of a place that will so well repay a visit as Caracas, or a country that is so well worth exploring as Venezuela. To a sports-

A CLEARING IN THE COUNTRY

man it is a paradise. You can shoot deer within six miles of the Opera-house, and in six hours beyond Macuto you can kill panther, and as many wild boars as you wish. No country in South America is richer in such natural products as cocoa, coffee, and sugar-cane. And in the interior there is a vast undiscovered and untouched territory waiting for the mining engineer, the professional hunter, and the breeder of cattle.

The government of Venezuela at the time of our visit to Caracas was greatly troubled on account of her boundary dispute with Great Britain, and her own somewhat hasty action in sending three foreign ministers out of the country for daring to criticise her tardiness in paying foreign debts and her neglect in not holding to the terms of concessions. These difficulties, the latter of which were entirely of her own making, were interesting to us as Americans, because the talk on all sides showed that in the event of a serious trouble with any foreign power Venezuela looked confidently to the United States for aid. Now, since President Cleveland's so-called " war " message has been written, she is naturally even more liable to go much further than she would dare go if she did not think the United States was back of her. Her belief in the sympathy of our government is also based on many friendly acts in the past: on the facts that General Miranda, the sol-

dier who preceded Bolivar, and who was a friend
of Hamilton, Fox, and Lafayette, first learned
to hope for the independence of South America
during the battle for independence in our own
country; that when the revolution began, in 1810,
it was from the United States that Venezuela
received her first war material; that two years
later, when the earthquake of 1812 destroyed
twenty thousand people, the United States Congress sent many ship-loads of flour to the survivors of the disaster; and that as late as 1888
our Congress again showed its good feeling by
authorizing the secretary of the navy to return
to Venezuela on a ship of war the body of General Paez, who died in exile in New York city,
and by appointing a committee of congressmen
and senators to represent the government at his
public funeral.

All of these expressions of good-will in the
past count for something as signs that the United States may be relied upon in the future, but
it is a question whether she will be willing to go
as far as Venezuela expects her to go. Venezuela's hope of aid, and her conviction, which
is shared by all the Central American republics,
that the United States is going to help her and
them in the hour of need, is based upon what
they believe to be the Monroe Doctrine. The
Monroe Doctrine as we understand it is a very
different thing from the Monroe Doctrine as they

THE CUYUNI RIVER

With View of the English Station that was sacked by Venezuelan Troops, and from which Inspector Barnes was taken Prisoner

understand it; and while their reading of it is not so important as long as we know what it means and enforce it, there is danger nevertheless in their way of looking at it, for, according to their point of view, the Monroe Doctrine is expected to cover a multitude of their sins. President Monroe said that we should "consider any attempt on the part of foreign powers to extend their system to any portion of this hemisphere as dangerous to our peace and safety, and that we could not view any interposition for the purpose of oppressing those governments that had declared their independence, or controlling in any other manner their destiny, by any European power, in any other light than as a manifestation of an unfriendly disposition to the United States."

He did not say that if a Central American republic banished a British consul, or if Venezuela told the foreign ministers to leave the country on the next steamer, that the United States would back them up with force of arms.

Admiral Meade's squadron touched at La Guayra while we were at the capital, the squadron visiting the port at that time in obedience to the schedule already laid out for it in Washington some months previous, just as a theatrical company plays a week's stand at the time and at the place arranged for it in advance by its agent, but the Venezuelans did not consider this, and believed that the squadron had been sent there to intimidate the British and to frighten the French and German men-of-war which were then expected in port to convey their dismissed ministers back to their own countries. One of the most intelligent men that I met in Caracas, and

VENEZUELAN STATION ON THE CUYUNI RIVER
The Barracks and House in which the English Police were confined

one closely connected with the Foreign Office, told me he had been to La Guayra to see our squadron, and that the admiral had placed his ships of war in the harbor in such a position that at a word he could blow the French and

German boats out of the water. I suggested to one Venezuelan that there were other ways of dismissing foreign ministers than that of telling them to pack up and get out of the country in a

ENGLISH STATION ON THE CUYUNI RIVER

Inspector Barnes, Chief of the English Police who were captured by the Venezuelan troops, is seated on the steps

week, and that I did not think the Monroe Doctrine meant that South American republics could affront foreign nations with impunity. He answered me by saying that the United States had aided Mexico when Maximilian tried to found an

19

empire in that country, and he could not see that the cases were not exactly similar.

They will, however, probably understand better what the Monroe Doctrine really is before their boundary dispute with Great Britain is settled, and Great Britain will probably know more about it also, for it is possible that there never was a case when the United States needed to watch her English cousins more closely than in this international dispute over the boundary-line between Venezuela and British Guiana. If England succeeds it means a loss to Venezuela of a territory as large as the State of New York, and of gold deposits which are believed to be the richest in South America, and, what is more important, it means the entire control by the English of the mouth and four hundred miles of the Orinoco River. The question is one of historical records and maps, and nothing else. Great Britain fell heir to the rights formerly possessed by Holland. Venezuela obtained by conquest the lands formerly owned by Spain. The problem to be solved is to find what were the possessions of Holland and Spain, and so settle what is to-day the territory of England and Venezuela. Year after year Great Britain has pushed her way westward, until she has advanced her claims over a territory of forty thousand square miles, and has included Barima Point at the entrance to the Orinoco. She has refused positively,

DR. PEDRO EZEQUIEL ROJAS
Minister of Foreign Affairs

through Lord Salisbury, to recede or to arbitrate, and it is impossible for any one at this writing to foretell what the outcome will be. If the Monroe Doctrine does not apply in this case, it has never meant anything in the past, and will not mean much in the future.

Personally, although the original Monroe Doctrine distinctly designates "this hemisphere," and not merely this continent, I cannot think the

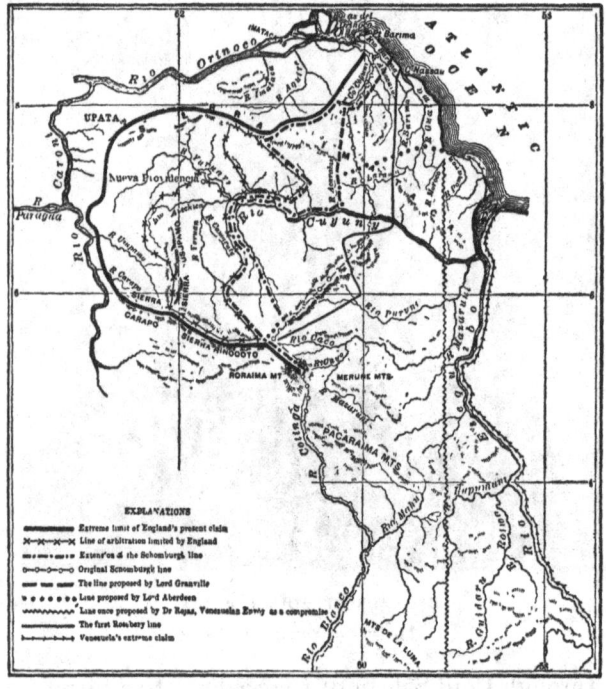

MAP EXPLAINING VENEZUELAN BOUNDARY DISPUTE

principle of this doctrine should be applied in this instance. For if it does apply, it could be extended to other disputes much farther south,

THE CITY OF CARACAS

and we might have every republic in South America calling on us for aid in matters which could in no possible way affect either the honor or the prosperity of our country.

In any event the Monroe Doctrine is distinctly a selfish one, so far, at least, as all rules for self-preservation must be selfish, and I should prefer to think that we are interfering in behalf of Venezuela, not because we ourselves are threatened by the encroachments of Great Britain, but because we cannot stand by and see a weak power put upon by one of the greatest. It may be true, as the foreign powers have pointed out, that the aggressions of Great Britain are none of our business, but as we have made them our business, it concerns no one except Great Britain and ourselves, and now having failed to avoid the entrance to a quarrel, and being in, we must bear ourselves so that the enemy may beware of us, and see that we issue forth again with honor, and without having stooped to the sin of war.

Caracas was the last city we visited on our tour, and perhaps it is just as well that this was so, for had we gone there in the first place we might have been in Caracas still. It is easy to understand why it is attractive. While you were slipping on icy pavements and drinking in pneumonia and the grippe, and while the air was filled with flying particles of ice and snow, and the fog-bound tugs on the East River were shrieking and screeching to each other all through the night, we were sitting out-of-doors in the Plaza de Bolivar, looking up at the big statue on its black marble pedestal, under the shade of green palms and in the moonlight, with a band of fifty pieces playing Spanish music, and hundreds of officers in gold uniforms, and pretty women with no covering to their heads but a lace mantilla, circling past in an endless chain of color and laughter and movement. Back of us beyond the trees the cafés sent out through their open fronts the noise of tinkling glasses and the click of the billiard-balls and a flood of colored light, and beyond us on the other side rose the towers and broad façade of the cathedral, white and ghostly in the moonlight, and with a single light swinging in the darkness through the open door.

In the opinion of three foreigners, Caracas deserves her title of the Paris of South America; and there was only one other title that appealed to us more as we saw the shores of La Guayra sink into the ocean behind us and her cloud-wrapped mountains disappear, and that, it is not necessary to explain, was "the Paris of North America," which stretches from Bowling Green to High Bridge.

THE END